ANOTHER STORY

ANOTHER STORY

Short Stories

by Emma Krasov

Writers Club Press
San Jose New York Lincoln Shanghai

Another Story
Short Stories

All Rights Reserved © 2002 by Emma Krasov

Writers Club Press
an imprint of iUniverse, Inc.

For information address:
iUniverse, Inc.
5220 S. 16th St., Suite 200
Lincoln, NE 68512
www.iuniverse.com

ISBN: 0-595-22384-2

Printed in the United States of America

Dedicated to the gentle memory of Murka, the observer cat. (1989–2001)

Contents

Acknowledgements

Thanks to my husband Yuri for his infallible support; to my son Yan for the first edit; to my daughter Alexandra for the last edit and the cover, and to my cat Matthew for playing my silent muse and staring at me when I write.

Run Your G-string Up The Flagpole And See If It's Perestroika

Unforgettable Happy School Years

1

Valya ran home through the dark and deserted streets. She ran so fast that finally she found herself up in the air, above the ground, between the electric lines. She almost reached the moon when familiar voices interrupted her flight and made her stop, and catch her breath, and half-open her eyes.

"Where am I supposed to get a ruble for you? I haven't got any money." Her mother yells in an outraged tone. "Here. Take this coin and cut it in half if you want."

"Why don't I ever have any money?" Valya's father yells back. "Where does all of it go? I feel like an idiot constantly borrowing from people. Can't I afford a pack of cigarettes?"

"Well, you are an idiot, you should feel like one. This time, try borrowing cigarettes instead of cash. Maybe it'll help."

Here we go again. Mom and Dad start another happy day at the Petrick residence. Lying on her old couch behind a fabric screen, Valya, a sophomore, hears them bickering, but makes no move to get up. Her mom's hand stretches from behind the screen and pulls off her blanket.

"Hurry up! You're gonna be late for school!"

"Gene, it's time to go!"

She turns to Valya's brother, a factory worker, who is shaving over the washbasin in the corner. The Petricks occupy one big room in a communal apartment where they share a kitchen and a bathroom with the neighbors.

After a scanty breakfast, Valya puts on her brown school uniform and a faded coat worn fall through spring. She takes her torn school bag, stitched with cord, and rushes through the dark corridor full of hangers, ladders, and bikes. Mom follows her, dressed no better, applying lipstick in the darkness, not bothering to look in a mirror.

"Wait, we'll go together."

"But Mom!"

"I said wait. I'll walk you to school. And after school you go straight home! Look at Novikova! Isn't it a shame? That won't happen to us."

Valya rushes downstairs trying to stay at least a step ahead of this embarrassing loud woman who happens to be her mother.

In routine school boredom, there is no place for dreams, or dreamers. Sitting in Russian literature class Valya barely listens to the teacher. Looking pensively through the rainy window, she sees electric lines that run from one invisible pole to another and remembers her dream…

"Our topic today is a summary of Eugene Onegin's character," drones the teacher. "Besenko, where is your plan summary? Let us see…Onegin is a philosopher. That's correct. He's bored with his village. That's right. Techenko, where is your notebook? Everybody, open your notebooks."

The teacher, in her dreary gray dress, slowly walks between the rows, glancing at the students' homework.

Valya opens her notebook and turns back to the window. All of a sudden, her very first day at school comes back to her mind. Maybe because her mom had mentioned Novikova, Valya's particular classmate…Ten years have passed since then, but she clearly remembers their first meeting; all the humiliating little details. In the principal's office, six-year-old Valya clung to the wall beside the door not daring to raise her eyes, while her mother yelled and squealed in the principal's face, waving her hands, demanding attention.

"What do you mean a magnet school? Why should I care that in your school they study English? We could do without English all right, but this school is on our block! Why should I place my kid at the school across the road if we live on this very block? I'd rather let her learn English in addition to Russian and Ukrainian in your fancy school, than be run over by that crazy traffic. The child will be crossing that road twice a day all by herself. We can't afford after school care, and I'm working full time, for God's sake! You know how our salaries are. Sorry, we are just uneducated blue collars. So what? Aren't we the same Soviet citizens? Do we still have our rights, our equality? I'm telling you, she's not going to any other school, but yours. And that's that!"

"O-o-h, calm down, Mrs. Petrick, calm down," the obese principal raises her puffy white hand, trying to stop this fury. "Your girl is poorly prepared. She'll never keep up."

"But I'm telling you—she will! You'll pull her through. What are the teachers here for?"

The door behind her opens quietly and yields a voluptuous pedigreed lady in a stylish dress, matching gloves, and expensive stilettos. She elegantly takes off her cat's eye sunglasses and turns to the door.

"Sweetie, come on in."

In the doorway appears a beautiful blond girl in pink, with a silk ribbon in her hair.

"Good morning! Here we are." Half-embracing her shoulders, the lady gently pushes her daughter forward. The principal raises her swaying body to greet them.

"Good morning, good morning, Mrs. Novikova!" She smiles. "You are all set. Your little Erena, she's Erena, isn't she?—Is now enrolled in the first grade. With the best of our educators, I assure you. Our Mrs. Smirnova is famous throughout the whole school district, trust me."

"Sounds excellent!" smiles Erena's mother, "In that case we won't take up any more of your time. We shall see you in September. Good-bye."

"Good-bye! Good-bye!" repeats the principal like a parrot, bowing. At the door, Erena casts a quick glance at miserable Valya, huddled against the green wall in her ill-fitting dress of the same color.

Valya stares back. They look like twins, separated at birth and grown in different worlds. Erena leaves, following her mother.

"So, now what?" Valya's mom asks threateningly, approaching the principal's desk. "Do you think I don't understand how you did that? Do you think you can fool me?"

"What are you talking about, Mrs. Petrick?" the principal starts sounding defensive. "All right, if you insist—I'll enroll her. But beware that your daughter will never keep up." She pulls out a thick folder, and unwillingly skims through the papers in it.

"To Mrs. Smirnova's class," prompts Mrs. Petrick in a stage whisper.

"We got her into the school. Isn't that good enough?"

"Do you want me to go to the Board of Education to fight for my rights?"

"Okay, okay," puckers the principal with disgust. "If you insist, let her go to Mrs. Smirnova. But remember, I warned you."

"Okay. I'm warned." With a triumphant look, she leaves the office holding her daughter tightly by the hand…

Valya moves her dreamy eyes off the window and looks at Novikova. After ten years, Erena hardly resembles that living doll in a pink dress. Only her radiant blue-gray eyes are still the same…The teacher, meanwhile, approaches.

"Now, Novikova, it is good that your summary is done. Well, you are a good student. But do you remember, Novikova, that we have a Comsomol meeting today after school, and that your situation is the topic of the meeting? And as a class tutor, I simply don't know what else can be said here!"

An instant silence falls in the classroom.

"Erena, I'm talking to you. I tried to discuss your situation with your parents—unsuccessfully. They don't seem to understand what's wrong with you. What else can I do? Should I go directly to your grandfather as the highest authority? But his guards wouldn't let me in, I guess…" The class moves and giggles.

"By the way, does he know about your shame? Huh, Novikova? Why are you so quiet? You are all probably concealing this matter from the old man, while he's working his tail off in Communist Party, taking care of the people!" The teacher's voice breaks hysterically. "What are you and your mother and father thinking, Erena? How can you still attend school, I'm asking you? And when will you stop coming here and shaming our school, tell me please? Stand up, Novikova! I am talking to you."

Erena stands up, amid loud laughter and hoots of derision from her classmates. She has an ideally oval face, a straight nose, and a shapely little mouth. She's wearing a curled ponytail, but pulled to the side, somehow sophisticated. In her small ears, shine two tiny diamonds. Her school uniform is neatly ironed, with a clean white collar. Her youthful figure unmistakably reveals that she is at least six months pregnant.

"Oh my God, oh my God," whispers the teacher in amazement as if she was hoping the pregnancy would dissolve. "Novikova, why are you still attending school?"

"Why shouldn't I?" asks Novikova confidently, raising her beautiful eyes to the teacher. "I like it here."

Yells of delight break in the classroom.

The teacher steps back in a shock. Suddenly she notices Valya with that distracted and joyful look on her face.

"What are *you* thinking about, Petrick? What are you smiling at?"

"Me?" Valya mumbles in confusion, "I was thinking about…when I met Novikova for the first time…"

"Oh, you were crazy about her!" follows a comment from the class.

"Kissy me, lezzy!"

"Roses are red, violets are blue."

"You are so sexy, I'm in love with you!"

"…we were both six years old," Valya continues in a low voice.

"And? So what!" yells the teacher impatiently, having lost all sense of the conversation.

"So…so I always wished I could be Erena Novikova!" bursts out Valya in despair. Her classmates are having a time of their life.

2

Erena opens her apartment door.

"Is that you, honey?" she hears from the depth of the long corridor.

"Yes, Mom."

Erena hangs her school bag on the hook and takes off her gray squirrel coat, wide enough to embrace her growing stomach.

Dim lights blaze in the corridor, a crystal lamp throws vibrant shadows on the soft vinyl wallpaper with decorative copper nails.

"So, what's new in school?" asks Erena's mother, smiling.

"Not much. We had a Comsomol meeting."

"Did they fire you from the Comsomol?"

"No. The teacher said I could stay on for Grandpa's sake…So, we just talked about young communists' responsibilities and left."

"I can imagine how amusing it was."

"Yeah, our class decided to raise money for a baby stroller."

"That's a riot! Okay, sweetheart, come change, and eat something. I bet you crave something salty. Smoked salmon or caviar?"

"Both, I guess, and…"

"All you can eat!" She kisses her daughter on the cheek. "Oh, yes! Alexei and his parents will be visiting tonight. Don't talk much about your school friends and all that stuff in front of them. They're very understanding, but since they are your future in-laws, the less they know about you, the better you'll get along with them."

"But Mom, I won't leave you and Daddy!"

"Of course you will, honey. When Alexei turns eighteen, and you are able to marry, your baby will be two years old. You won't need my help any more. You'll get married then and move to your own place. Daddy will make sure it'll be in one of those new improved buildings that all the Central Committee wives are so crazy about. But remember, your mother-in-law can get to you anywhere."

The doorbell rings unexpectedly, and Mother hurries into the corridor. Erena changes in her cozy bedroom. She pulls out a white fuzzy bathrobe from her three-door closet and turns on a tape recorder that starts playing "All You Need is Love."

Having picked up an orange from a crystal bowl on her bedside table, Erena heads to the living room. Her grandfather, just arrived, is taking off his suit jacket. He is a solid top-level governmental officer with a very straight spine, neatly combed gray hair, and a healthy blush on his cheeks.

"Hey, Grandpa!" Erena approaches with a smile. "Are you staying?"

"Hello there! I've got a short break between meetings. Tell your mom I won't eat. She said you've hired a new maid?"

"Yeah. We have a Natasha now. She's quite a cook!"

"Anyway. I'd rather take a nap." He briskly moves through the room and makes himself comfortable on a white leather sofa.

"Grandpa," Erena nibbles on a piece of orange, "what was your specialty?"

"What do you mean by 'was'?" he says, looking suspiciously from behind the pages of *Pravda*. "Why 'was'? I'm still here! I still have a specialty."

"I mean your education. What kind of profession did you study for? I guess they didn't call it the Communist Party Leaders course? At least, I've never heard of one. What was your major?"

"Oh, that's what you mean! It was…well…Marxist-Leninist Logic."

"So, do you remember anything from your studies?"

"Of course, I do." He gets red-faced. "Well, we studied…a lot, a lot…Oh! How about this: do you know anything about the law of cause and effect? Well, this is logic. And one of those French men from the, well, seventeenth or eighteenth, or nineteenth century, that great philosopher, you know…this famous what's-his-name…Anyway, he made this tremendous logic statement. Listen carefully now. 'A teakettle put on the fire, cannot get covered with ice.' See, I still remember."

"Uh-huh," says Erena politely. "Very impressive."

3

Valya comes back from school to the usual neighbors' quarrel.

"Look at you! I just leave the kitchen, and you immediately shut the window. You can fry eggs on the floor, it's so hot in here! Well, some people just can't stand any fresh air."

"But you're no better, you've turned on the radio and left it blaring. You sit in your room and what are we supposed to do? Plug our ears?"

Another neighbor passes Valya, heading to the kitchen, and her voice adds to the choir.

"Look, he's drumming already, and now his sister's home. I bet she'll take over the bathroom again and then you can kiss it goodbye!"

"This is not a home, it's a mad house, honest to God!"

From the Petricks' room, a loud drumming resounds. Valya opens the door and sees a familiar picture—her brother Gene, a member of the amateur band of his factory, ears plugged, beats the drum, marked "Trade Union Property". Gene, with his eyes shut in deep delight, yells at the top of his lungs, "O-bla-di! O-bla-da! Life goes on, bra!"

Valya pulls out a box of instruments used in drawing class, and picks the one that resembles tweezers with its split, springy end. She hides in the bathroom. First, she studies her face in an old murky mirror over the sink. Then she tries to arrange her straight disobedient hair in different ways. She turns in profile, right and left—this is her face all right—neither beautiful, nor ugly, everything is utterly common. Narrow gray eyes with thick eyebrows. Lips…Her lips definitely could be more expressive. Valya digs in a neighbor's cabinet over the bathtub. Ah, a tube of old lipstick! What else? A short black eyeliner pencil, filthy from soap or chalk. Valya washes it off and draws the contour of her eyes roughly, unskillfully. She puts some lipstick on and pushes her lips forward as if for a kiss, bows her head, raises her eyes, and assumes a love-me-tender look. Her teeth glow.

Someone knocks at the door. "Are you done?" a neighbor yells. In response she turns on the hot water and hurriedly washes her face. She takes the tweezer-like drawing instrument and starts to pluck her eyebrows furiously, biting her lip and wrinkling her nose in pain. This is not the first time, but she is still not used to it. Damned eyebrows grow with incredible speed, and fighting them back threatens to become a daily problem. This time she has worked so hard that her eyebrows now look like two thin treads. Underneath them, the skin is red and swollen.

Valya goes back to her room and sits on her old couch. She pulls out a small mirror. After thoroughly studying her face, she decides that some more improvements can be made, and locks herself in the bathroom again, this time with scissors. In a moment, bangs hang over her forehead. They are too short due to a miscalculation, yet very daring.

4

Through the dark streets of downtown, lit by store windows and street lamps, passes a long black automobile, quickly and soundlessly. Erena's grandpa returns home, to the suburbs, after his workday. Crowded streetcars and trolley buses are passing by, with passengers' bags and coats squeezed in the doors.

In the darkness, Grandpa's car enters a neat suburban town and glides to an old park with a modern mansion in its depths. Tall gates quietly open and close behind the car.

5

Late at night, Valya's mother returns home. Neighbors' voices sound from the kitchen. TVs and radios scream from every room. Dragging her heavy shopping bag, she asks her son:

"Is Dad home?"

"Nope", answers Gene, chewing on a cold hot dog and watching TV. "He got overtime."

"Oh, that's very good. And Valya? Hey, Valya!"

"What?" asks Valya, writing at the dining table.

"Are you doing your homework? Fine. Gene, sonny, what are you chewing on? A cold hot dog? Let me at least cook it for you!"

Mother heads toward the kitchen. Gene continues to turn knobs of an old black-and-white dim TV in a futile attempt to get a better picture.

Returning with a hot pan, Mom pushes away Valya's books.

"That's enough, daughter. Let's eat. What? What's this?" she looks closely at Valya's face and throws the pan on the table so hard that the cooked hot dogs jump out, falling on the floor.

"What have you done to yourself? What the hell is this? Bang cutting? Eyebrow plucking? You little slut! Are you a whore like Novikova? Look at you, you little piece of trash! No! Anything but this! That will never happen here!"

Valya bursts into tears and runs behind the screen to her old couch. She covers her ears madly, whispering curses. Through the crack in the screen she can see how her mother pushes her school books off the table, and her brother fidgets with the TV set, too used to such family scenes to intrude.

6

In the bright morning sunlight, pouring through dusty windows, a student, named Serenko lingers at the blackboard, struggling with the Ukrainian literature assignment. The rest of the class, happily out of the teacher's attention, is involved in unrelated activities. Valya opens a textbook and places a small mirror between the pages. Leaning over the desk, she licks her fingers and restlessly rubs her freshly plucked eyebrows. Her new bangs insolently stick out over her forehead.

The mousy teacher in a plain gray dress and thick glasses pronounces slowly.

"Continue, Serenko, I'm listening to you."

"So, in his…in his own…in his 'Caucasus' poem, Shevchenko, the poet, showed, well, so, he showed that Russia used to be…" mumbles Serenko.

"Russia used to be a *prison for the nations*," the teacher interrupts. "That's right, Serenko, in the time of the czars, Russia was like a prison for all the nations on its territory. Don't be so shy at the blackboard, Serenko. Take your seat."

She turns to the class. "And now, children, each of you will write a summary of the poem privately. I will collect your assignments in ten minutes. Ivanenko, why are you peering into Besenko's notebook? I said you write it privately. Put away all the unrelated objects, children. Petrick, what are you doing?"

Valya hides her mirror and opens a notebook. For a while all are thinking hard, chewing on their pens. Just before the bell rings, a folded note falls on Valya's desk. While everybody jumps up, handing the assignment to the teacher, Valya anxiously reads the note.

Her next class is History. There are slogans on the walls: *Marxism is not a dogma, but a direction for the action,* and *To study, to study and to study more—Lenin.* The school principal, who teaches History, walks among the desks. Valya does not hear her slow quiet speech. She's reading the precious note once again.

"Valya, I'll leave school pretty soon, so I want to invite some folks to a farewell party. Would you tell the boys and some nice girls to join? Saturday after school my parents won't be at

home, and our maid is off. I have music and everything. I'll
wait.
Erena Novikova."

Valya instinctively covers the note when the teacher's voice approaches, but the voice turns to her:

"And Russia used to be…what, Petrick? What did Russia use to be at the time of the czars?"

"Russia used to be a prison for the nations," standing up to answer, reports Valya without a second thought.

"No! Russia used to be *the granary of all of Europe!*" the principal corrects her in an outraged tone. "Take a seat, Valya, shame on you! What are you thinking about?"

7

At night on her old couch Valya tosses and turns. Sleep escapes her. The window is too bright. Her brother's snoring is too loud. She hears her parents' whispers:

"Tomorrow is payday. We must buy some meat to store in the freezer, and we don't have any potatoes, either."

"I know, I know."

"Yeah, yeah. You know everything. You can do anything. So why can't we make ends meet?"

"Look, Ma, just stop it. You want me to remind you about that stupid pair of pantyhose you bought a month ago? If it wasn't for that, we could still have some pork in the fridge. Am I right? Okay, forget it. Hey, move over a bit. What is this leg doing here?"

Valya gradually falls asleep to the quiet squeaking of her parents' bed.

She becomes a gorgeous angel-girl in gauzy clothes, white and blue, like in ancient art. Her hair is golden and wavy. She feels its warmth on her cheeks. Yet something warms her even more—a sunset. It shines right in her eyes, but does not blind her. A sweet beautiful music sounds from the skies. Valya raises her face up to the sky, and starts to sing. She sings a strange heavenly melody and she flies higher and higher. The sun is down now, under her feet, she soars into the blue, and her beautiful clothes soar behind, and suddenly right into her streams an unbelievably bright light.

The white glow approaches, and from the middle of it appears her reflection, the same beautiful airy girl with long golden hair, and in a transparent white outfit. She comes closer—Valya knows her. This is her precious friend, Erena Novikova!

Valya hurries toward her, so she can take her hand, or kiss her. She wants to desperately. But Erena's hand is bodiless. It disappears. Her face laughs, but it dissolves, dissolves, and Valya catches emptiness. The sun goes out. It is getting cold. The magical music stops, and Valya wakes up. She fumbles near the couch in search of her lost blanket. Then, wrapped in it tightly, she shuts her eyes, hoping to dive into the shiny dream once more.

8

Dim gray dawn gradually lights a beautiful suburban house, surrounded by old trees. A spot of sunlight rests on a bronze bust in the center of the park. The metal face looks noble and willful, with a thoughtful furrow in the brow. This is the image of Erena's grandfather, Vasiliy Vasilich, immortalized in a sculpture in front of his own mansion.

An early bird emerges from within the house—Vasiliy Vasilich in a fancy *Adidas* jogging suit. He makes his usual ten circles around the bust, breathing out clouds and getting a ruby-red glow on his cheeks. Suddenly a shameless pigeon from a nearby branch drops a greenish "hello" right on the bronze nose of the noble statue. Sharp-eyed Grandpa jogs over to his own monument and pulls out a snow-white handkerchief. He rubs the damaged spot until it shines even more than before. In the process, Vasiliy Vasilich drops his wallet. He carefully picks it up, and needlessly checks all of its precious contents: Communist Party membership ticket, deputy ID, Soviet passport, all his special passes and personal invitations.

He turns his eyes to the house, and sees in the first floor window a maid with white lace on her head. She watches him, and signals with a handkerchief that the master has finished his morning exercises; it is time to fill the bathtub and prepare breakfast.

9

On Saturday, after the usual school day, Valya's classmates gather in the hallway. Erena Novikova was taken home earlier by her father's personal driver, but all the students know that today she's home alone and expecting them for a party. They gather their saved lunch money and head to a neighborhood liquor store. Cheap ports and table wines are always available in abundance.

"Valya, what do we take? 'Red Ink' or the 'Mighty White?'" asks the money keeper.

"Both," she replies joyfully, "and all you can eat!"

They buy several bottles and hide them in their school bags. They are in high spirits all the way to Erena's home, located downtown in the depths of a quiet yard, full of neatly cut bushes.

Erena in a maternity dress opens the door. Her classmates are being thoroughly impressed with the ambiance of the luxurious apartment.

"Cool, look at this!"

"Wow! What a place!"

"Hey Erena, aren't you lucky! I wish I had parents like yours! How many bedrooms do you have? Ten?"

"Look at this! Is it a kitchen? I thought it was a conference hall!"

"Let's go to the living room," invites Erena. "There is music there and a VCR."

"A VCR? No kidding? Wow! That should be something!"

"So what? They've had this stuff abroad for years now. Besides, remember who her grandpa is? Right, Erena?"

The crowd heads to the living room, which has a shaggy carpet and puffy pillows around a coffee table.

"Girls, perhaps, you'd like to change?" offers Erena. "I have something for everybody in my bedroom."

The girls follow her with a scream of excitement. In front of a wide-open wardrobe, they are stunned for a moment, then they grab the hangers with glamorous outfits.

"Look! Labels!"

"Everything is made abroad!" they whisper in admiration, shamelessly taking off their boring brown school dresses. Only then do they realize that what they are wearing underneath is not quite French lingerie. Their rough domestic undershirts, ugly bras and insanely colored panties contrast too sharply with those heavenly outfits—a black nylon blouse, a gray suede miniskirt, a floral pair of jeans, a fuzzy low-cut sweater in fluorescent pink.

Erena politely turns away, allowing her friends to get rid of extra underwear, so it will not mar the lines of the perfectly cut clothes.

"Girls, I have something else for you," says Erena, enjoying her role of a fairy. "Let's go to my mom's bedroom."

A screaming group plunges into a luxurious, carpeted and curtained bedroom in maroon. There in front of a huge mirror beckon shiny jars and boxes with perfume, nail polish, powder, eye shadows, blushes, and lipsticks.

"And it's all imported. Unbelievable!"

"This is not imported," corrects Erena. "Imported means something made abroad, and sold here. But you can't get *these* things here. They all are from the outside. My mom and dad don't shop here." Erena does not want to brag, and looks at the silent girls hesitantly. "Valya, can I talk to you in private?" she says, catching Valya's adoring and envious look. "Excuse us."

Erena takes Valya back to her bedroom.

"Look, Valya, you are such a good friend…I know you were never gossiping about me. You never hated me for what I am…unlike others. I just want to give you something. This is nothing, actually, these things are too small for me now, anyway."

She digs into the drawer of her finely crafted dresser, and pulls out a slim beige bra and matching panties, all covered with lace.

"Go ahead, take it. Put it on and enjoy."

"No, no, Erena, my mom will kill me!" mutters Valya, accepting the gifts with her trembling, parted fingers. "In all my life I've never owned anything like this!"

"Now you do!" answers Erena enjoying her embarrassment. "And if you're afraid of your mom, just don't tell her anything. Keep them in your school bag!"

"Oh, Erena, thank you so much," whispers Valya through tears, following Erena to the maroon bedroom again, where all the girls are deeply involved in putting on makeup. Valya hastily joins them.

"Hey, wait, I'll help you," offers Erena. She takes a cosmetic brush from Valya's hand, and carefully places layer after layer on Valya's simple face: foundation, powder, eye shadow, blusher.

"That makes a difference," she says, admiring her own job. "You've got some color in your face." Erena grabs a metal hairbrush. "Only your hair remains. Wait…"

A curling iron is plugged in. Erena takes Valya's bangs and neatly curls them underneath. She makes big curls on her head. Putting the curling iron aside, she brushes Valya's hair twice.

"Now look!"

The girls sigh enviously behind her back. Valya stares at the mirror, hardly believing that this sultry goddess is herself.

"What do you think?" asks Erena. "That my hair is wavy as it is? And my lashes are naturally black? And my nails shine by themselves? The thing is, I cannot do it as brightly for school. So I use mild colors, light lipstick, clear nail polish. Practice makes perfect."

Everybody laughs.

"Lucky you, Erena!" sighs one of the girls. "Your parents give you everything!"

"It's my grandpa," explains Erena. "My grandpa gave everything to my parents. They gave it to me, and I'll give all this to my baby. If my grandpa still holds on to his leading party position, of course."

Erena strokes her rounded stomach. Embarrassed at her gesture, the girls hurry to get back to the living room, where *The Beatles* play and the boys are finishing their second bottle of wine.

"Hey look at our girls!"

"No, way! Just look at these babes!"

"Where is your Comsomol modesty?" The boys are utterly astonished.

Erena places a plate of exotic oranges and bananas on the table. The fun continues.

"Guys, I'll turn on the VCR, sh-h-h very quietly," Erena puts her finger over her lips. "My parents actually don't let me watch X-rated. But Alexei, my friend and I, we do, when they aren't home. We'll make it mute, in case someone comes."

Erena slides the videotape into the VCR and turns on the screen. After a couple of close-ups of brightly painted young faces, the screen starts flashing naked bodies in a variety of interlacing. With their mouths agape, Erena's classmates forget everything, watching the movie. Those faded porn photos that circulate through the school once in awhile do not even compare to this "piece of art."

Early twilight fills the room. After the video, the boys start to drink again. They decide to stay in darkness. Random couples form and gradually dissolve in the huge dark apartment, and only sighs and whispers are heard. Erena peels an orange in a rocking chair, left alone in the living room, deep in her thoughts.

Valya sits on the edge of a huge bathtub. With wide eyes, she follows black and pink tiles, shiny mirrors, palm trees in buckets, rows and rows of perfume and shampoo bottles on the wide glass shelf. She recalls the peeled dirty blue paint and eternally damp ceiling in the communal bathroom of her home, rust spots on the bathtub, a neighbor's basin, always full of soaking dirty linen, washtubs and rubbing boards on the walls. How can some people be so lucky when others are so miserable? She deeply inhales the smells of luxury, closing her eyes, forgetting everything. The door quietly opens, and a boy, who lacks a girl in the classmates' orgy, sneaks in. He sits close to Valya, and suddenly hugs her and starts kissing her face, mumbling and moaning.

"You jerk, get out of here!" screams Valya, and pushes him hard. The poor guy falls into the empty bathtub, pulling Valya along. Unexpectedly amused she calms down, and lets him hug her again. They flounder in the bathtub for a while, so that Valya's hairdo and makeup are hopelessly damaged.

Erena awakes from her self-absorption only after having finished the orange. She stands up and turns on lights.

"Hey people," she shouts to the corridor. "Who wants to smoke? We can do it in my dad's den."

She heads to the other end of the apartment, and opens a double door to the den, decorated with ancient arms, bronze, and marble figurines. Deer and wild boars' heads are mounted over the couch and armchairs. There is a bear's hide on the floor. Red-faced boys and disheveled girls appear from the different corners of the huge apartment. Everyone wants to sit on the bear's skin. Valya modestly sits on the edge of an armchair. She dreamily strokes the hunter green velvet upholstery. Erena pulls out a pack of slim brown cigarettes and graciously offers them to her friends. In a minute, a fog of smoke fills the den. A sudden ring of the doorbell makes everybody shudder and rush to the crystal ashtray.

"It's okay, it's okay," Erena tries to comfort them, slightly worried herself. "Sit still, I'll be right back."

In silence and darkness, no one dares to move, while Erena opens the front door. It's her grandpa.

"Hi there. Is your mom at home?"

"Hi, Grandpa. She and daddy are out, remember? And I have guests."

"Who? Alexei?" asks Grandpa, taking off his coat. He sees an unusual number of coats and jackets on the hangers. They look too worn and faded for this place. He asks more harshly.

"Who's here, Erena?"

"Grandpa! They are my classmates. I should at least say good bye to them before I leave school. This is my farewell party." Trying to change the subject, she asks, "Why are you still in the city? It's night, you should be at home."

"Well, my dog had surgery today. I wanted to pick him up, but the doctor said, in two hours or so. He wants to see how anesthesia effects him. The doctor is the best, according to our comrades with dogs, so everything should be fine, but you know, I still worry. Find me something soothing in your mom's medicine cabinet. I'll go lay down in the living room."

Grandpa makes himself comfortable on the sofa with the *Pravda* in his hands. Erena leaves to find him a tranquilizer.

"It's just my grandpa." She informs her friends in the den. "Why are you so quiet? He's having a nap, so we can still have fun. Only hush!"

Yet while sitting still in the darkness, her friends have realized they do not belong in this world, and have decided to leave. On their tip-toes, the girls come back to Erena's bedroom, quickly and quietly. Avoiding looking at each other, they change back into their hated school dresses. The boys are awkwardly hanging around in the lobby. Erena dusts off cigarette ashes from the armchairs in her dad's den.

Valya, who has changed first, slips out of the bedroom and heads to the bathroom, but slows near the half-opened door to the dark living room. She listens to a load rhythmic snoring for a second, feeling only her own heartbeat. Then, suffocating from anxiety, she quickly opens the door and steps inside. In twilight, she sees an old man sleeping on the sofa, his newspaper on the floor, his suit jacket hanging on the chair. Two soundless steps and Valya is standing next to him. She is kneeling, studying the face, so familiar from the media photos. She smells those rich perfumes, not imported, not sold here, but brought from abroad. Suddenly she stands up. She quickly slides her hand into every pocket of the old man's suit jacket on the chair. In a moment, she holds his thick leather wallet in her hands. She puts it in her school dress pocket, and quietly goes to the bathroom.

In the corridor, the boys and girls are ready to go. Erena knocks at the bathroom door.

"I'm coming, I'm coming," replies Valya. "I have to wash off my makeup. I can't go home like this!"

She turns on the water and quickly goes through the documents in the wallet. Then she hides it again and splashes some water onto her face. When she joins her friends, they all take off from the enchanted apartment.

When Valya comes home, her brother Gene is enthusiastically watching the TV series *Good Night, Kiddies,* looking at the dancing puppets over his drum. To Valya's relief, her parents are not home yet. She sits on her old couch, opens her school bag, and examines her new treasures, delighted and proud of herself as never before.

10

The next morning, Sunday, in Valya's communal apartment the radio loudly sings *Good Morning, Good Morning, What A Wonderful Day*—the theme song of a Sunday program. A foul steam oozing from the kitchen fills the whole apartment. On the communal stove, as usual, one neighbor is cooking dinner in advance for a big family; another is boiling bleach and dirty bed linen in a huge bucket. A washing machine buzzes in the bathroom, and rinsed linen splashes in a gigantic basin under running water.

Gene is loudly snoring, sprawled out on his cot. Valya feverishly dresses—she is in a hurry.

"Val, go buy some milk. Now!" yells her mom.

That suits her just fine. Still pale after sleep, Valya quickly leaves home with the empty milk bottles. Not far from the store, she quickly looks around and hides in a solitary telephone booth off the pavement. She hangs her shopping bag on the hook, pulls the stolen wallet from her pocket, and finds a business card. She carefully reads the telephone number marked *home* and takes damp coins from her clenched fist.

"Hello," she starts in a husky voice. "Is this Vasiliy Vasilich?"

"Who's calling?" asks a courteous woman's voice on the phone.

"It's me…you don't know me…well, tell him, that I have found his wallet."

"Wait a minute, please. I'm transferring you."

"Speaking," a solid man's voice answers.

"Vasiliy Vasilich, good morning," mutters Valya, loosing her breath.

"Who's calling?"

"Vasiliy Vasilich, my name is Valya. I'm from your granddaughter Erena's class. Yesterday we were at her place and you just came when we were leaving. I left first, because I was in a hurry. I found your wallet in the elevator. And not until I reached home did I look in it and realize it was yours."

"That's good. Very good. Where do you live? I'll send my chauffeur now."

"Oh, no, no!" Valya objects, forgetting that argument is not appropriate with this sort of person. "I don't want to give it to your driver, but to you personally, please. I can only give it to you personally. Not now. I can't now. Tonight. Tonight at six. Vasiliy, please?"

"First of all, you are supposed to call me by my *full* name—Vasiliy Vasilich—under any circumstances, ever." He is clearly annoyed with her impudence. "Secondly, I'm making a big exception letting you give me another call tonight. But remember that I know your name and where you are from. My people can reach you if necessary. So, it would be better for you not to play games."

"Oh, no! Yes! Thank you, thank you, Vasiliy Vasilich," hurries Valya, not realizing that he had hung up the phone.

11

Erena answers the doorbell and stares at Valya—people do not visit this home without an invitation.

"Erena, hi! I…" Valya says, embarrassed, "I've just come for a minute. May I?"

Erena remains silent.

"I," Valya continues, "I'd like to ask you…Oh, sorry…are your folks at home?"

"Nope," finally utters Erena, studying Valya, "but I expect Alexei any minute now. Well, what do you want?"

"I…if it won't hurt, I wanted to ask you if…if…I could put on some makeup of yours. See, tonight I have a very special date…in a special place…and I really have to look my best, you know…"

"Okay, then," Erena interrupts her ingratiating babbling. "I understand. Come on in, you can put my makeup on your face. But hurry, he's coming soon, and he doesn't like it if someone else has my attention."

"Of course, of course," Valya whispers, taking off her faded pea-colored coat. She is wearing her best outfit, a cheap, yet fashionably cut, velveteen dress. She had to lie to her mother that she was invited to a birthday party. She has "a gift"—a couple of books, wrapped in white paper. Valya puts them on a chair in the vestibule. In her mini dress and patterned pantyhose, she looks older, more feminine.

Erena warns her again.

"Look, don't take long."

She softly closes the door behind her. With trembling hands, Valya grabs some powder, blusher, and eye shadows. Only after she spills some on her dress, does she regain control and calm down. She makes her best seductive face, rolls up her eyes, smiles, becoming the image she desires, and then, with confident sharp strokes makes up her face, perhaps overdoing it a bit.

She hears the melody of a doorbell and Erena's low cheerful voice, and the high insolent voice of Erena's boyfriend, Alexei, the only child of his well-to-do parents. She calmly continues her business. Erena passes down the corridor to the kitchen with the words:

"I'll bring it now."

One can hear crystal tolling and metal pealing, the soft bang of the fridge door. Alexei shouts from the corridor:

"Hey, Erena, heat some stew in the microwave, will ya? I'm quite hungry."

"Fine," she replies from the kitchen. A soft sound of the oven door follows.

On his way back to the living room, Alexei sees a light under the maroon bedroom door and opens it sharply. For a moment, he stands motionless, not expecting to see Valya here. Scared a little, she takes control of things first and tries to squeeze herself past Alexei into the corridor. Alexei is tall, athletic, strong. He presses Valya to the doorframe, quickly grabbing her behind with both hands. Valya recoils, but has no luck escaping. Alexei grabs her tighter, and in a moment, easily throws her onto a huge bed with a satin maroon comforter. Silently, efficiently, he pulls up Valya's dress. She is not wearing pantyhose, but stockings attached to a tight corset, which embraces her from the waist down to the tops of her legs. He tries unsuccessfully to pull it off. It does not budge, an armored rubber-ized domestically produced quality corset. Alexei loses the initiative.

Valya slides away from under him, quickly leaps to her feet, and dashes to the door.

"You, trash!" hisses Alexei to her back. "Change your pretty outfit before you come to my wife's home. Rags are not allowed here!"

Valya anxiously pulls on her coat, barely managing to get her arms into the sleeves. Rolling a serving table in front of her, Erena appears from the kitchen.

"Leaving so soon, Valya?" she asks courteously, while Alexei sneaks behind her back from the bedroom to the living room.

"Yeah, I've got to go. Thank you, Erena," Valya smiles with trembling lips.

"Anything wrong? Your package is here. Don't forget." Erena points to the books wrapped in white paper.

"Oh, those are for you. A gift." Valya stumbles.

"For me?" Erena laughs sweetly. "Oh well, thank you." Looking at disheveled Valya she asks again, "Are you okay? What happened?"

Pressed to say something, Valya squeezes out,

"I always wanted to ask you…"

"What?"

"Aren't you embarrassed? To walk around…this way?"

"Nope!" Erena smiles, turning up her little nose. "I'm a woman now, not a stupid virgin. Look at me, it's obvious! Isn't it cool?"

They laugh, although constrained, and Erena opens the door wide for Valya.

"Bye-bye!"

On her way to the living room, Erena unwraps the gift. The upper book is by Hemingway. She is not curious enough to look at the other one.

"Poor girl," she shows them to Alexei. "I'm sure she sacrificed the best from her own bookshelf. Hasn't she noticed that we've got more than enough of these?"

Furiously Alexei rips the books from her hand and quickly tears them to pieces, throwing their vinyl covers far away into the corner.

"I don't want to see that trash in the house anymore! Do you understand?" he whispers menacingly, coming closer to Erena. "You are my wife, is that clear?"

Erena shrugs and turns to get her serving table from the corridor. She opens the door to her mom's bedroom and glances at the messed up bed. In a moment, she serves food to her future husband, smiling calmly.

12

At six, Valya huddles in a drafty telephone booth with broken windows, dialing the sacred number again.

"Hello, Vasiliy Vasilich! Yes, it's me, Valya. No, I haven't changed my mind. I'll give it only to you, personally. Yes, please. I'll be standing there."

She rounds the corner and stands in an open windy place in front of a big movie theater. She shifts from one foot to the other, tapping the pavement with her worn shoes. Anxious, she does not realize that the long black car stops for her. She is watched for awhile from behind the tinted windows. Then the door opens and the driver, walking around the car, helps Valya into the back seat. She almost disappears in its enormity.

The gigantic automobile starts easily. The etched, tanned face of Erena's grandfather half-turns to Valya.

"So," a well-groomed elderly hand with transparent manicured nails stretches impatiently.

"Not now, please Vasiliy Vasilich," mumbles Valya, firm in her decision to make things happen. "Not here…I'll give it to you, personally."

"Ah-h…What's that? What do you want me to do for you?" asks the majestic old man, unsuccessfully trying to view Valya, lost in the far corner of the back seat.

"I...I want to go to your place, Vasiliy Vasilich...to visit...to be your guest," pronounces Valya with a sinking heart. "And there I will give you what I have."

"Hmm. All right then," he whispers, turning to the driver. "Home."

When at home, Vasiliy Vasilich quickly leaves her alone. The driver sees Valya to the door, where two muscular young men take her inside. In a second, they unbutton her coat and rapidly search her from both sides, simultaneously squatting, so she only realizes it is a search when the old man's wallet emerges in the hand of one of them.

A maid appears soundlessly and whispers something to the guard with the wallet. He nods, puts it into Valya's hands, and turns her softly to the entrance.

The maid leads Valya through the huge hall to the stairway, then to the second floor, and leaves her there, opening the door to a luxurious den.

"Please wait," she says and hurries downstairs.

Valya gathers all her remaining courage and enters the den, lit only by the bright street light outside the window. She sits on a velvet sofa.

An enormous Great Dane noiselessly appears, sniffs Valya, and disappears.

The maid comes again with some bottles, glasses, and a box of chocolates on a serving table. On her way out, she turns on a nightlight. Valya does not move. Minutes of silence and solitude pass. Finally she rises from the sofa, glances into the corridor, and tightly closes the door.

At the end of the corridor, Vasiliy Vasilich arrives. He has changed out of his suit jacket with the deputy pin and into a casual silk shirt. Only his facial expression has not changed—the haughty and scornful look of a people's servant.

Clearing his throat, he opens the door to the den, but no one is there. He enters, looks around in confusion then notices a strange little hut on one of the armchairs, made from the opened pages of *Pravda*. The hut moves slightly, then from under the paper a girl's hand stretches out, with the precious bulging wallet. A shadow of a smile lightens the stern look of the old man. He takes the wallet. He cannot help but open it immediately and check. Everything's in its place.

The newspapers meanwhile collapse and reveal Valya curled in the armchair, almost naked, dressed in Erena's translucent gifts, and with a desperate smile on her brightly painted face. Valya's clothes pile up under the chair, covered with her wrinkled drab coat and a crease-resistant domestically produced corset.

"Oh, look at you, little rascal," says Vasiliy Vasilich sounding absolutely sincere. "Have you decided to entertain me?" he seems genuinely touched. Valya stands up in the chair, and smiling more broadly, suddenly asks.

"Do I look like a French woman?"

Amused, Vasiliy Vasilich helps her to step down. He attempts a kiss, but only slides his dry elderly lips over the young generously blushed cheek, and not knowing what else to do, he fills two cocktail glasses with Finnish lemon vodka. Valya gracefully accepts a glass and timidly takes a sip.

"So," mumbles the old man, examining Valya from head to toes, "nice figure." After this remark prolonged silence hangs. Valya huddles, feeling cold. Vasiliy Vasilich sits in an armchair and she immediately slides onto his lap. He seems afraid to touch Valya with his hands, yet he finishes his drink, places his glass on the table, and then hugs her tightly. The "lovers" spend a couple of awkward minutes in this position. Then, releasing the embrace, Vasiliy Vasilich offers Valya a box of chocolates. She takes a fancy candy and puts it aside. He gets busy with the stereo system, trying to put on some music, though he takes much longer than it would be necessary.

Valya is getting colder. She decisively stretches out on the sofa. The old man approaches, and again tries either to kiss her, or to demonstrate the quality of his shaving on Valya's cheek. Then, changing his mind, he stands up.

Valya, understanding that her last chance is slipping away, assertively draws the gray head to her mouth and kisses it with all the passion and ardor of youth.

"I'll take you on as staff…As a nurse, do you want it?" he mumbles, trying to escape.

"Mother will kill me," between the two kisses Valya replies, trying to unfasten her bra with one hand.

"I'll marry you off to the Committee," whispers Vasiliy Vasilich.

"To whom?"

"To KGB. Let her try to kill you then, ha-ha!"

Valya finally manages to take her bra off and throws it as far as possible, but her victory is far from final. Vasiliy Vasilich, now disheveled and red-faced, leaves the sofa again to fill his glass. Enjoying Valya's look from afar, he finally says.

"I'll take you. You are the right person. I like you. Why don't you drink?" He finishes his second drink.

Chilled to the bone, Valya in her lace panties gets up from the sofa and silently collects her clothes. She puts them on, hearing as if in a dream, "You know the phone number. Just call. On the fifth. No, better on the tenth…of the next month. I'll do as I promise."

He accompanies Valya to the stairs. She playfully smiles and waves to him, holding back desperate tears that burn her eyes from inside.

Wonderful Restless Youth

1

Erena's apartment is illuminated by all of its lamps and chandeliers, despite the summer afternoon's brightness. Natasha, the maid, gives orders to the newly hired waitresses, who run from the kitchen to the living room where a big dinner table is set, shining with crystal and silver. In the long corridor, Erena's mom and some female relatives chase a cute little girl, who carries in her pudgy little hands a big crystal bowl, full of early strawberries, very close to being dropped on the floor.

"Lucy, honey, stop, my little sweetie, give this bowl to Granny," begs Erena's mom, catching the girl at the door. The child throws the bowl away with a loud cry. The telephone rings. Erena's mom picks up.

"Hello. He's not here yet. No, you can't talk to him. No, please do not call later. Who died? He was demoted last month, wasn't he? Oh, okay, I know him. Well, yes, I understand, but today is our daughter's wedding. Yes, yes, you, guys, wait until Monday. All the Central Committee is gone for the weekend anyway. Bye!"

She hangs up and runs to the circle of aunts and waitresses formed around little Lucy who is crying over a puddle of strawberries. Squeezed by all her relatives in turn, she ends up in the arms of her granny, who presses the child to her enormous bosom until Lucy starts screaming and kicking, pushing away from the smothering chest.

A doorbell interrupts these comforting caresses. The newlyweds arrive, Erena in her ivory gown, with heavy flowers in her hands, and Alexei, now wider in the shoulders, but with the same impudent expression on his face. Following them is Erena's daddy and a few sophisticated guests. They join the crowd and disappear in the endless apartment. In her white bedroom Erena, even more beautiful than two years ago, hugs and kisses her screaming daughter Lucy in adoration. The child barely escapes to find herself in her grandpa's hands and after that into the hands of her own rather too young father. She's taken to the guests and passed from hand to hand. Gaiety increases after they sit around the shining table. As crystal and silver ring, happy exclamations resound, reaching little Lucy's bedroom, far down the hall. There, in the pink light of waving curtains, she sits in her lacy dress on a pink carpet and cruelly tears a big, beautiful, blue-eyed doll to pieces.

2

Vasiliy Vasilich rests in his home office, now completely redecorated. The old sofa is gone, replaced by a wide luxurious bed. He pushes the button of the intercom and calls only one word.

"Nurse."

A bright blonde easily runs upstairs in her stilettos and a snow-white uniform. She slips through the half-opened door and right there, in the doorway, takes off her nurse gown, under which there is only a slim black garter belt with a pair of net stockings. She hardly resembles that desperate schoolgirl. Bleached hair, neat make up…wide smile…Now she *does* look like a "French woman" indeed. Valya nonchalantly sits on the bed, Indian style. She stretches out her hand and pulls *Pravda* from the desk. She unfolds it and monotonously reads in a loud voice.

"Letters from our readers. 'I cannot bear not to share my pure joy with you, my dear favorite newspaper. I am a gray-haired veteran, and I was given a new Soviet passport today—a red-skinned little book—as the poet has called it. My wife Galina, and my daughter Maria, and my granddaughter Daria also received their new passports. Our happiness has no limits.'"

While Valya is reading, her boss quietly sits on the bed and starts stroking her net stockings and her bare hips, until Valya's voice falters and stops…

3

In Erena's apartment, the celebration is in full swing. Alexei hugs his smiling bride, flushing from too much alcohol. The guests chat and laugh while waiting for new dishes. Music is playing, waitresses slip around. The maid Natasha picks up little Lucy, who fell asleep in her chair and carefully carries her back to her bedroom.

The doorbell rings and the bride cries out.

"Grandpa!"

Everyone rises. People here know how to honor the head of the family—the one, who gave everything to them. The most impatient guests flow out into the corridor. Erena runs around the table in a hurry to hang on the neck of Vasiliy Vasilich. On his arm rests Valya's neatly manicured hand with a marriage band on her finger. Behind them, there are two inexpressive muscular young men, one of them is Valya's young husband, Kolya, a KGB officer.

When the newly arrived sit at the table, Alexei looks over his wife's shoulder and asks indifferently, glancing at Valya.

"Who's the slut?"

"Don't you recognize her? You've met," Erena grins ironically. Alexei raises his eyebrows. Erena explains.

"She is that 'trash' you ordered me not to let into the house a couple of years ago." Erena sincerely enjoys her husband's amazement. "What? Sour grapes?"

"Well, it's not too late…" Alexei stares at Valya. She turns away.

"Go ahead," encourages Erena.

"Watch me." Alexei finishes his champagne, pretending not to notice Valya's anxious look. He slowly, almost unwillingly rises from his chair, picks up a pack of *Kent*, and leaves the living room.

Erena turns to Valya.

"Valya, be so kind, bring me my white purse from my bedroom, since you're sitting closer. I want to show you Lucy's pictures."

Valya readily stands up, but approaching the door to Erena's bedroom, she hesitates. The moment she walks in, Alexei, who is hiding behind the door, promptly closes it and stands in Valya's way.

"So, you are trapped now!" he says with a drunken grin. Yet Valya doesn't seem embarrassed. For a minute she looks straight into his eyes, and then starts undressing herself, grabbing and lifting the hem of her gleaming maroon dress, showing her net stockings and bare white thighs. She takes her dress off very slowly, giving Alexei time to keep up. At the same time, she is backing to the open window behind the silk white curtains. Alexei quickly takes off his pants. Before his next move, Valya, still in her dress, grabs his pants and throws them through the open window. Her casual laughter is gloating.

"So…trash," she coyly addresses Alexei. "Where are your designer trousers now?"

She dashes out of the bedroom and calmly walks back to the feast.

4

Valya and her husband Kolya work and live in Vasiliy Vasilich's mansion. Such an arrangement allows little free time. Their only night off, they spend in Valya's parents' place. It is no longer a gloomy blue-walled communal apartment. Now it is a spacious four-bedroom of their own in a new building. Valya's mother cannot brag enough about her daughter's success—great paying job, a young KGB officer for a husband, and she got an apartment for the whole family.

However, the Petricks hardly enjoy it. All year round, they have country relatives visiting. They flock to the city to shop at any season. Out-of-towners sleep in every room, so Valya and Kolya are placed in the same bedroom with her parents and brother Gene.

At midnight, the guests are still scampering through the rooms, loudly stamping with their bare feet and talking. Gene is already snoring on his cot, now in use again. Valya's parents are having their usual fight scolding each other for being disrespectful to their respective relatives.

Valya hugs her young and healthy husband on her old couch behind the worn out screen. They do not feel cramped.

"Do you want to?" she whispers, pressing harder against his body.

"I do," he replies in a whisper, stroking Valya's back. "Know what?" he decides to take action. "Let's go drink some water."

They tiptoe to the kitchen. The sound of snoring overwhelms the entire apartment.

"Or, maybe, let's do it now in the bathroom?" offers Kolya.

"No! Someone will sure creep up. Don't you know them? They're always thirsty after vodka. Better drink some water. At three in the morning it'll wake you up, just like an alarm clock."

Valya's husband fills a big jar with tap water up to the brim, and hands it to her. She drinks, and drinks, but stops in the middle.

"That's all, I can't take any more."

"Go ahead, finish it, or you'll sleep till morning. Drink to the bottom."

With great effort, Valya finishes the jar, and panting watches her husband drinking.

"It's better in your own bed, isn't it?" she encourages him, sliding her arms around his waist. "We'll be up at three, go to pee, and be able to make love while they all sleep. Till six, if you please. Just push me if you wake up before me, okay?"

Hugging each other, they quietly go back to their couch.

In the morning, Valya rests in a bubble bath. The loud voices of her mother and relatives come from the kitchen. Mother offers those rare treats that are now available to her family through Valya's occupation.

"Try this cod liver, and the marinated mushrooms! Aren't they good? Have you ever seen a ham this pink? The cheese is so fresh, it smells like flowers! It's all Valya. If it wouldn't be for her government job, we would still be eating sawdust and living in that communal mad house. Hey, Gene, come out here, get some cured meat before your father wakes up. He'll grab the best pieces! Eat it up, sonny, it's time to go to work."

Relatives noisily approve Valya and her top job, so profitable and pleasant for all.

"Kolya!" calls Valya's mother. "Come out here, get something yummy. Your wife is still soaking! It's like an addiction. She's bathing day and night, like a duck. Come here, Kolya, here's some caviar. Try some new potatoes with dill and butter. Why are you turning up your nose? You'll work hard for the whole week in that castle, no one's gonna treat you there like your mother-in-law!"

Despite her offers, Kolya leaves the breakfast table and shyly scratches on the bathroom door. Valya unlocks it. Slapping her bare behind, Kolya laughs gladly.

"Kolya," Valya steps back, returning to the fragrant bath. "This bathroom is too small. These boring white tiles, this old mirror, this puny basin...I can't stand seeing it any more. We should rebuild it. Like Erena's—a little pool, and all in pink and black. I've always dreamed about having a bathroom like that, you know?"

"Uh, why not?" Kolya is in a good mood. He catches his wife's legs under the water. "If you want, we'll rebuild it. Only we'll have to deepen the wall, and it's a lot of noise. There are neighbors there." He doubtfully observes the bathroom.

"So what?" impatiently asks Valya. "It's not like it will go on for ages. We can hire someone for good money to do it faster. Look." Valya stands up, and shows precisely where they should take out a part of the wall to widen the bathroom. She takes a massage brush on a long handle and knocks at the wall here and there.

Behind the wall of Valya's bathroom, there is a neighbors' bedroom. In it, a balding stocky man looks under the bed for his socks, which he took off yesterday. His wife, Zena, in a slip and a white blouse, but without a skirt yet, bends over the low-hanging mirror to unroll her hair. Sharp resounding knocks on the wall disrupt her.

"She knocks, that whore! Does she knock for you?" with her hands over the rollers, she turns to her husband.

"What?" he is genuinely puzzled. Red-faced from his extended search, he suspiciously sniffs the sock, discovered under the bed.

"Don't you know what? Don't you hear Petricks' little slut knocking? She slept over at her parents, that Central Committee hooker!"

"Oh! You mean little Valya."

"Valya, Valya! Cat Vasiliy's pussycat! What are you grinning at? What's so funny? These bitches have everything, and we, the honest people, nothing!"

"Why are they bitches? Why are they necessarily bitches? This girl has a top Communist party job. So what? Are you jealous? It's clear that they won't take the crooked and hunchbacked for that job."

"Oh, you are such an ass! A Communist party sucker! That's what you are. They prosper on your party membership payments, don't you realize? Don't you know whose money has paid for Vasiliy's servants, for his whores?"

"So what? He is in power. He *is* power. They are supposed to live better than us."

"Says who? If it weren't for your and other fools' membership payments to the Communist party, your filthy leaders wouldn't ever have all that luxury. They've never worked, never earned a penny. They get everything for nothing, those "servants of the people." Why the hell do they live way-*way* better than their masters, the people? Houses, mansions, cars, garages, security, cooks, maids, gardeners! And we can't even dream of getting a car, even with our own, hard-earned money."

Zena's husband pulls on his socks and rolls up his eyes disapprovingly, but Zena is not going to stop anytime soon. "We work, but we can't buy a thing. They "lead," and they get it all! The best colleges, tours abroad, Black Sea resorts. Even furniture and clothes, gas and electricity, telephones—everything is just *given* to them for being our leaders. Who do you think pays for all that? *You do!* You pay, and they all enjoy. They, and their bitches, and the old Petricks, and their little slut. All of them!"

"To hell with them!" Finally erupts her husband. "I don't give a shit! I'm even glad that such a girl can live on my party payments. Let her! I'd give her my salary if she would live with me too. Do you understand you nag? Bite me! Look at you. You're ho-o-o-o-nest! Your fucking honesty isn't worth a rat's ass!"

"And yours! And what about yours?" lashes back Zena, ripping out her rollers. "Who are you? Are you the one who gets the money? You spout hot air in the plant's Communist party bureau every night for nothing. You'd better get some paid overtime job. But why bother if you have me? I'm going blind from typing day in and day out at work and on the side. You're their prey! And look at them. They get life. They enjoy! They have those girls and all the privileges, and you are left drooling. So pay your little payments for them and continue to drool, you Communist party puppet. You honest working fool!"

"Look, you jabber too much! During Stalin, you would be dead for just thinking this way. Be grateful that you are safe and sound you stupid bitch! And don't forget that we've gotten our privileges, too. If I hadn't joined the Communist party, we would have never gotten an apartment in *this* building. So, there."

Angrily storming out into the hall, Zena grabs her purse to rush to work. But feeling that the final chord has not yet sounded, she returns, rips off her wedding ring, and silently throws it into her husband's face. Glancing at her wristwatch, she tousles her hair with her fingers, and runs to the stairs, slamming the door, not noticing that she is running to work without a skirt. Outside she catches sight of an astonished Valya. Valya is dressed up, nicely coifed, and is sitting beside her husband in the long luxurious car of Vasiliy Vasilich, parked right in front of the door. The angry woman loses her last restraint, and gives Valya the finger, then madly rushes to the bus stop.

5

In the research firm building, made of glass and cement, sun shines through freshly washed windows. Inside, thousands of employees bustle about, creating a small indoor town with its own population, morality, values, and gossip. Two dozen women, who work in the Department of Information, stop their chitchat and courteously greet their boss as she arrives at the door in the company of two elegant strangers. Those two obviously do not belong to the work world, with their designer clothes and sophisticated makeup. The "worker bees" wake up early and commute to work before being able to primp. The typical outfit of the department editors and proofreaders during the hot summer consists of cheap T-shirts with childish prints and pseudo-denim skirts.

The younger girls look modish, though. They wear *Sassoon* haircuts, bright makeup despite the early hour, and they have those expensive platform shoes. Yet even they can't compare with this young lady, who's casually examining their boring desks and the hanging pots from which dusty ivies crawl down.

Erena Novikova, accompanied by her mom, meets the watchful glances of these younger women. She smiles at them and immediately gets smiles in return, while her mom explains to the Department's manager:

"The Minister of Agriculture, my husband's very close friend, said that my daughter could be employed with a company like yours, in the Department of Information, as a whatever-you-call-it staff member. Or, in the general Reception area as a Director's secretary. But, I don't know, really...Secretary sounds too busy. It'll be too much work for my girl, I guess. But in your Department of Information...there are too many people..."

"Oh no, no," babbles the boss. "It only looks like too many. This is not that bad. Our collective is very friendly."

"Col-lec-tive," repeats Erena's mother, sighing with her mighty bosom, on which a string of pearls glimmers, half-covered with gray chiffon. "Oh, well, we'll think it over. Thank you."

Throwing their czar-like good-bye to the "collective", the superior creatures depart. Shortly after, a tempest of exclamations begins.

"Was that her? The daughter of Vasiliy Vasilich? And that one—is she the granddaughter?"

"You can tell they're blue blood!"

"But what will she do here? Do they ever go to work, like us?"

"Of course not! They go to the Moscow University first, just for fun. Then they get married and go abroad with their hubbies! Am I right?"

"She can't go to the University, people say. She didn't even graduate from high-school because she had a baby!"

"How could it be? Do such things even happen to them?"

"Uh-huh! Especially to them. Cause they can get away with anything. They've got power, they've got money. They don't need morals!"

"Oh ple-e-ase!" the younger girls try to defend a person of their own age. "It's not like you weren't the same when you were young!"

"Who? Us?" the elder women exclaim with outrage.

Word by word the discussion becomes more detailed:

"The girl is beautiful, I have to say, but her bosom is somewhat…insignificant."

"Yeah, unlike her mom's!"

"But what an outfit!"

"Yeah, chic de Paris! Girls, let's make some coffee," offers one of the youngest.

"Fine. Then bring some water," others agree. A girl takes a jug and leaves for the bathroom. Following her with a glance, one of the women notices aloud.

"Her eyes are red. Perhaps, she's been crying again this morning. That husband, what a beast! Poor girl."

"I'm still thinking," starts another woman, studying her daughter's picture on her desk, "what if I had married a different man, then I would have had an absolutely different child…A prettier one."

She pulls out a folder and says, "Don't pour the coffee without me. I like it with foam. I'll be right back."

The moment the door closes after her, there comes a comment from the far desk.

"She likes her coffee with foam, what insolence!"

"Girls, who's seen her husband? Nobody? He's a cripple. He's limping!"

"No, it's not her husband, but Zena's, the typist's! By the way, where is she?"

"She's late, as usual."

"No, no! Zena's husband almost married a hunchback woman once, but he himself is not at all crippled! Just bald."

Everybody laughs.

"Who was that hunchback woman?"

"Don't you know? Oh, yeah, you can't know this. It happened in the good old days. Zena's husband went abroad for a whole year on a business trip. In those days, all our folks were sent abroad—in Algeria, in Tunisia…those were golden times. Half of our firm went there to build a dam or a drainage system, or whatever. Remember everybody talking how the Minister of Agriculture's son bathed that girl Helena in a tub of champagne? And when they came back, Helena happened to occupy the desk beside his wife, Olga. What a riot! Olga was sitting like this, and staring at Helena all day long, doing nothing. So, Helena got sick and tired of those looks, she went to the Director and told him about it, and he separated them, sending both to different departments. But that was the son of a Minister, so he got away with it. There's another story about Mr. Boyko. It almost cost him a Communist Party membership. He found a mistress there, too!"

After these words, one of the women, obese, badly dressed, and disheveled, stands up and leaves, slamming the door. For a moment, everybody keeps silent.

"Aren't you ignorant!" someone reproaches the speaker. "'Mr. Boyko found a mistress there…' That was her—our Luda!" She points at the door.

"Oh really? I didn't know!" the gossip replies, embarrassed.

"Of course you didn't know. Don't talk then. Let *me* tell you, *I* know. Mr. Boyko found a mistress there. And it happened to be nobody else but our little Luda. You must know, though, that in her younger days she was absolutely gorgeous, unlike now. She was pleasantly plump, with those full legs, always in black stockings, nicely dressed, neat and clean…she was such a peach! Little by little, she and Mr. Boyko got closer, and before you knew it, they were at it like rabbits! They drove everywhere together, took pictures, and never hid. So everybody knew. And her fiancé broke up with her. Guess who that was? Our Vice-Director of Science. Yes, yes, just imagine! Sure, at that time he was no Vice-Director. He was just like us, simple. Poor Luda miscalculated. Yeah, and Boyko, he had a wife at that time. You know her; she works in the Drainage. That bony redhead…always in good clothes. So, when they came back from that business trip Mr. Boyko said to his wife, let's divorce. But she went to the Director, and he called Boyko and told him, 'Either put your Communist Party membership ticket on the table or go back to your wife and don't ever say a word about Luda again.' That's how it was. And now, when Boyko comes to our department, he doesn't even say hello to Luda. Doesn't even look at her, as if he doesn't recognize her. And she got so fat because she got a slow metabolism from all her troubles. She ripped all her Parisian undershirts up for dust rags. That's the end of her love story."

"She'd better sell her Parisian rags to me," says one of the girls with a sigh.

She gets up and plugs the coffee maker in.

"Hey, so what was with Zena's husband?" recalls someone. "How did he almost marry a hunchback?"

"Oh, right!" the first speaker pops up, glad that she can take the floor now. "During that same business trip he met a Moscovite, an interpreter. She was hunchbacked. They had an affair there, abroad. You know, a long trip, and lack of women, all that. But he was far from taking it seriously. Anyway, some kind souls brought it to Zena. Only she was smart enough to take him back. That's why she has a husband now, while our poor Luda suffers alone."

From the back door, the boss appears from her office. All the women immediately bend over their desks in silence. Only the coffee maker sizzles. Fat Luda returns and sits at her place. The boss announces that she has a meeting with the trade union committee, and leaves, and the woman who likes foam on her coffee now comes back.

Not even taking a seat, she starts. "Girls, do you know where our Tatyana went? To the trade union committee office! There are packages for trips abroad there. Before they announced this, they called all the department bosses to let them choose the best trips, before the simple people would take them."

"Oh, we are fed up with 'abroad'" one of the elder women says. "We hear such horrors about those trips abroad..."

"By the way, how about our boss, Tatyana? Didn't she go on those business trips at that time? She's one who would be remembered!"

"She's remembered enough here."

"What are you talking about? Tell us! Tell us!"

"Come on!" plead others. "See, it's eleven o'clock now, time for our exercise break anyway."

"Yeah, tell us, and I'll pour coffee for everybody," promises one of the younger girls.

The women open their lunch bags, taking out their homemade snacks and sandwiches.

"Girls, who's going to the bookstore during the lunch break?" asks one of them, chewing. "Ask if they have those new books for recycling coupons. I've collected tons of them. You know what it takes to haul the old papers on your own back to that eternally closed recycling center, and to wait in line, and to come back for the stupid coupons! And after *all that,* the book store never gets the damn books!"

"No, I'm going to the grocery store—another line to stand in!"

"I'm going to catch the shoe repairman. He is usually drunk after hours, you know. So, take care of your books yourself. And take a closer look at those coupons. Usually they expire before you get them!"

Fat Luda pulls out half a loaf of bread from her faded tote bag, then a pound of salted pork in wax paper, and a jar of horseradish. Everyone starts eating. Tatyana, the boss, a full-figured woman of forty-something, with an aged doll's face and childish blond curls, returns from the trade union committee with a big envelope in her hand. She angrily looks at the eaters, her blue eyes sparkle. She opens her mouth, but Luda starts first.

"Oh, Tatyana! You're just in time! Would you like a bite?" she extends a gigantic sandwich in her boss's direction. "Try it. This pork is so fresh! And the horseradish is so sharp. You'll like it!"

Tatyana's eyes turn wild.

"Don't you know, Luda, that I'm on diet since yesterday?" She sharply turns around and slams the office door behind her.

Everyone looks at poor Luda.

"She ate it yesterday…" Luda mumbles defensively.

"Oh well," says one of the girls. "Forget about approaching her now. She's mad as hell. Damn, I wanted to ask her to let me leave early today. Tough luck! Who knows how long her diet will last this time."

"Don't worry," says another one. "It never lasts long. Remember her tomato diet? She quit after two days. Or that rice-and-milk one? It lasted from lunch till dusk. Then she ate all of Luda's leftovers, and a moldy muffin from my drawer, and everything was fine again!"

"Yeah, but I need to leave early *today*..."

"Go get her some pastry from the cafeteria, she'll never resist!"

"It's expensive though."

"But it's cheaper than cognac. That's what I brought her when I needed to go meet my boyfriend at the airport."

"So, what about Tatyana's adventures? You never told us!" reminds one of the younger girls.

The speaker opens her mouth but is interrupted by a longtime department resident:

"Will you stop? I'm sick and tired of your endless gossiping. Who doesn't know about Tatyana? All the company was buzzing about her at the time. That's enough!"

"It was buzzing before we were here," object the girls. "We don't know a thing."

"So," the speaker gets inspired again. Chewing on her piece of sausage, she continues. "Our Tatyana in her younger years was just a..."

"A peach!" helps the youth.

"Exactly. All the Ministry of Agriculture was hers. But she loved the President of the trade union committee. He was from the Caucasus, a Georgian. One hunky piece of man-meat, I'm telling you!"

"Oh yeah, they're so hot, those Southerners!"

"Exactly. So they were dating, but suddenly it was all over. Once he came on a date wearing that stupid Georgian-style *airdrome* cap and our Tatyana cut the relationship off—he looked way non-European! He was shocked, he couldn't understand what was wrong. He begged her to come back, but she said, 'You can take a guy out of Georgia, but you can't take Georgia out of the guy.' But he was such a stud. He didn't stay single for long. Another lady started flirting with him right away. Galya, a fluffy blond from Accounting, do you know her? She had a husband, two kids, but no apartment. And at that time the trade union was allocating apartments in a new building. So, every day she showed up in a new dress, with a hairdo, with a manicure, and visited him in his office. She said she was manicuring herself till two in the morning to look tip-top. And finally, she got to him. Seduced him. And they were seeing each other in that old busybody Belenko's place. She's the one from Personnel, that old witch. She also wanted an apartment in the new building. So, she would let them use her place for dates, hoping to get a new apartment out of the deal. And another old fart—Ivanov, the one who has driven a *Pobeda* for the last thirty years, he used to follow the 'love birds' and watch them, since they were conveniently dating during lunch breaks. They'd go to Belenko's place, close to here, just around the corner. And Ivanov would drive there and eavesdrop from behind the door. Then he informed the union board about their misbehavior, and he mentioned all the dirty words they used in bed. They were disciplined, of course, and stuck in their old apartments, but comrade Ivanov got a new one for being so loyal."

Loud laughter praises the speaker.

"Hey, girls, whose coffee is this?" asks one of the women.

"Zena's still absent. And her coffee is freezing. Oh boy, coffee is expensive now, twenty rubles! Why has it jumped so high?"

"Because of frost in Brazil."

"Frost in Brazil? There is no frost out there. I wish I lived in Brazil! Summer all year round, and the beaches. I'd look good in a grass skirt."

The door springs open and Zena, the typist, appears.

"Oh, girls," she is panting. "Just imagine what happened to me this morning! I forgot to wear my skirt and I only noticed it here, in the elevator. I had to run all the way back home for it. Isn't that awful? Is Tatyana here? She left? Oh, thank goodness! Maybe she won't notice that I'm late."

Amidst the loud laughter of her co-workers, Zena sits at her desk with a typewriter on it. One of the elder women, frowning, leaves the room.

"She is going to squeal on us," a comment follows.

The women pack away their food leftovers. They get ready to dash out of the building at the sound of lunch break bell.

6

Gene comes back from the factory to the same clamor in the Petricks' apartment full of their country relatives. Piles of packages and bags clog the hallway. Half-dressed people hang around a bottomless bottle of homemade whiskey set on the kitchen table. Opened cans and half-eaten delicacies are scattered all around. Gene picks on the leftovers, drinks some water straight from the faucet, and departs to the family bedroom where the huge trade union drum sits grandly in the middle of everything. About to start his routine rehearsing he is interrupted by a telephone call.

"Yes?" he says in a deep voice. "Valya? What's up? Who's coming to town? Oh my God! To hire a band here? You're kidding me! But how do you know? Uh-huh! And Vasiliy Vasilich can help me get there? Cool! Sure, I'll be there, *Moscow* hotel. Yeah, yeah, I'll dress up, don't fret! Okay, I got it—no drumming, he'll just look at me. I'll wait in the hall, all right. But how can he recognize me? Oh, yeah, I'll recognize him. I'm coming! Thanks a bunch, sis!"

Loud noises from the bathroom, where workers are destroying the wall, drown out his last words.

Slightly dazed from joy, Gene quickly puts on his best outfit—jeans, a denim jacket, and a pair of heavy platform shoes. After a quick thought, he adds a light nylon windbreaker. It's hot outside and this is too much, but the windbreaker is so cool—one of Valya's latest gifts.

In a posh hotel lobby, Gene tries to attract as little attention as possible. Even though he reported a minute ago that he's waiting for a job interview with a famous musician staying in the hotel, the beady-eyed doorman vigilantly watches him.

Finally, the doorman's attention is distracted by the arrival of guests. Gene turns away and watches a painter with a bucket coming from the stairway. The smell of fresh paint is filling the hall. A cloakroom man gestures to the painter to come closer. The painter leaves his bucket near the elevator and engages into a lively conversation with the cloakroom man. Then he counts and gives him some money, getting a package in return. The painter disappears behind the "Staff Only" door with the package. A group of Japanese guests heads toward the elevator, but all this slips past Gene's attention. He tensely observes the lobby, trying to find among the faces that one which will be his guiding star in the dream world of professional musicians.

The Japanese guests enter the elevator. The lobby is empty and the piercing eyes of the doorman drill into Gene again. He starts sweating in the denim and nylon. Embarrassed, he finds a pack of cigarettes in his pocket and starts smoking. As if he were just waiting for this, the doorman approaches.

"No smoking here. You need to put that out."

Gene looks around for a trashcan, and notices a bucket near the elevator. He throws his cigarette in it. A pillar of fire flies up from the bucket of oil paint. The doorman freezes in shock. Gene almost faints. In a moment he swiftly pulls off his nylon windbreaker, and throws it over the bucket, trying to put out the fire. The windbreaker bursts into flames in his hands. A Japanese guest, lagging behind his group and waiting for the elevator, courteously steps aside. When the elevator door opens, Gene throws his burning windbreaker in. The paint bucket falls and flaming paint leaks on the floor, adding to the cataclysm. The elevator shaft is rapidly engulfed in fire.

7

On a Sunday morning, Zena and her husband are awakened by a loud knock from the Petricks' apartment.

"Their impudence has no limits!" wails Zena, throwing off her blanket. She jumps out of the bed and beats the wall with her fists.

"Get up," she yells at her husband. "Enough sleep for today. We gotta hang the rug on this stupid wall! Now! We've been living here for a year, in this stupid building, and you still haven't hung up the rug!"

"Why the rug? What about the rug?" her husband is pulling the blanket back, trying to return to his peaceful Sunday morning sleep.

"Hang the rug up, I'm telling you, so I won't hear that stupid noise. I can't live with this madness! For the whole week she's been knocking and knocking on the wall, that stupid bitch!"

"Oh, shut the hell up, don't start again, you tick!" the husband wrinkles his face, understanding that there will not be any more sleep. "These are cement walls," he explains weakly, searching for his socks under the bed. "I'll have to use a drill. Then the wooden corks…It's a lot of hassle."

"I don't care! Whatever it takes. Stop the noise! They've became too insolent, those Central Committee ass-kissers. Hang up the rug. Now!"

Zena rushes to the closet. Showing a supernatural physical might, she drags out a giant rolled up Oriental rug, the true pride of a simple Soviet family. Her husband wearily plugs in the drill.

Behind the wall, in Valya's bathroom, two sweaty workmen just finished setting tiles. The numerous population of the Petricks' apartment is still asleep. Only Valya, in a cloud of pink nylon, leans by the door, and watches their job with a smile. Now everything looks exactly as she wants it to. Black and pink tiles are covering the bathroom wall, standing much deeper now than before.

She makes a gesture, inviting the workmen to the kitchen table where a light breakfast is served. Cheese, ham, tomatoes, and a jar of homemade whiskey. Valya returns to the bathroom and turns on the hot water.

"Don't rush, lady," one of the workers says, chewing. "Let it dry."

Valya turns back to the kitchen. With a dreamy smile on her face, she pours herself a cup of coffee. She does not notice the workmen's glances, evaluating her in her pink nylon, wondering if it is possible for a man to have a bodily contact with such an airy figure. As soon as they are done eating she impatiently sees them to the door, sticking money in their hands.

Zena's husband is standing on a ladder dressed only in his boxers. He is making holes in the wall under Zena's supervision. Many holes are needed, and they have to be wide, too. Wooden corks will go into the holes, and strong nails will be nestled in the corks to handle the weight of their prized possession, the heavy bright-red patterned rug.

"Too high," commands Zena. "That hole is much lower. Move a bit sideways, or it will be too big."

"Oh, shut up, you pest. I know what I'm doing."

"Of course, you know. You know everything. You can do everything. Then why do we still have nothing? No nice furniture, no decent TV or stereo. Why can't you bring anything home, like other people do?"

"Other people have their wives to bring everything."

"Oh yeah? Their wives? You mean like Valya, those kinds of wives? There you go again with your whore. Go kiss her ass! She knocks days and nights, she disturbs people's sleep, and you don't care. She can do everything, sure, she's Vasiliy's cheap pussycat, a trashy slut! And you tell me to be like that scum."

Pushing into the wall with all his strength, her husband tries to cover Zena's violent outburst with the noise of the drill.

After the workmen are gone, Valya idly drifts through the apartment for awhile. Everyone is still sleeping. Her new bathroom pulls her like a magnet. Hesitatingly she turns on the water. Clouds of steam cover the shiny tiles and the mirror, built in the wall. Having filled up the tub, Valya dissolves a bottle of fragrant bubbles in it and takes off her pink peignoir. With sheer enjoyment, she soaks in the hot water. She shuts her eyes, dozes off, and listens to the neighbor's drill with a serene smile. Soon the heavy rhythmical blows follow. At first, they do not trouble Valya at all, then the sounds become suspiciously too loud, and the sweating tiles seem to shake and move under the hefty quakes.

"Kolya!" screams Valya in horror. "Kolya, come here. Hurry!"

The wall shakes harder. Having constricted herself in a lump, Valya crawls further in the corner of the tub. The furious banging increases. In a cloud of dust, Kolya breaks through the bathroom door at the very moment that Zena's husband, followed by his wife's scream, crashes through the wet wall, falling directly into the tub full of bubbles. Zena's face freezes, her mouth wide open as Valya's bare legs fly up into the air, splashing bubbly foam onto the ceiling. Behind Kolya's back, Gene is covering his face with burnt hands in thick bandages.

Decline Of the Communist Empire

1

On one of the last days of summer, warm and windy, with a scent of dust and dry leaves, a luxurious black car drives up to the school building. An attentive chauffeur opens the door for a stunning young lady, dressed in a white suit appropriate to the season. After her, out of the car dashes a fair-haired child in a denim skirt and white socks, her mommy's little carbon copy.

They head to the principal's office. The principal—a colorless male of indeterminate age—jumps up from his seat and, with a half-bow, hurries to inform.

"Don't you worry, Ms. Novikova. You should not have troubled yourself to come here. Your Lucy has been enrolled in the first grade."

"Thank you," replies Erena with dignity. "We don't dare detain you any further."

She gently pushes Lucy toward the door, charmingly smiles at the principal, and leaves the building, silent and freshly painted before the new school year.

2

Any workday in the Department of Information starts with makeup and coffee. The population of the Department is the same as four years ago, but with some new young faces as well. In the midst of the usual morning chitchat the door opens sharply, and Zena, out of breath, bursts into the room.

"Erena's not here?" she nods toward the "Head of the Department" door.

"No, she's not," one of the women replies. "Take a seat, cool down. We'll have some coffee now. Zena, do you remember Nina? I was just telling the girls about her. That one, who slept with Alla's husband in Alla's own apartment?"

"Of course I remember," says Zena. "She used to work at the Irrigation. Alla would run to the stores during her lunch break, seeking food for her family like a good wife, and Nina, with Alla's husband, would go to their home on a date."

"Wait, let me tell it," interrupts the woman who started the story. "They went there separately. And Nina tried on all of Alla's dresses and she and the hubby made fun of Alla. When she came back after lunch, she took her seat near Alla, because they were best friends and their desks were beside each other. So, Nina told Alla all about her 'boyfriend,' not mentioning his name, of course, and how *hot* he was, and all that. Alla in turn told her how *frigid* her husband had become lately. Can you imagine!"

The younger girls' laughter fills the room.

One of them, newly hired, asks unexpectedly.

"Hey, girls, who would stick her bare ass out of the window for a thousand rubles?"

A hail of laughter follows and only fat Luda grumpily retorts.

"There are no girls here, Angela. There are only ladies."

Yet Angela's idle question begets a new conversation.

"I could," says one of the girls. "Only not on the first floor. Or someone would touch it."

"So what?"

"It should be more expensive. That's what."

"I would never do such a thing," says an elder woman gravely. "That would be such a shame!"

"Who cares about shame? Making money with your bare ass is not a shame. This is 'labor heroism.' But to live with a bare ass like we do, that's a shame!"

The younger ones are having fun.

"And who would sleep with comrade Slenev for a thousand?" Angela just cannot stop, naming the trade union librarian, a moss-covered veteran of the company.

"Ugh!"

"Never!"

"Not for a fortune! That could leave you frigid till the end of your life!"

"But I could try," one of the girls muses. "I would cover myself with a silicate glue...wait until it dries...and it would make sort of a diving suit on me. And in *this* I could even go under comrade Slenev!"

"You didn't consider that he would sweat and all your glue would melt," laughs Angela, "if he would manage to climb on top of you, of course!"

The young girls laugh themselves to tears.

"Aren't you girls ashamed? So young and so outspoken! Now Erena is coming, and you didn't even touch your work yet!"

As if she were waiting just for these words, snow-white Erena Novikova sails through the door. She charmingly greets her subordinates and dashes to her office in her high heels.

In the silence resounds Angela's comment, "What a gal! Crisp and cool!"

At that moment, the radio signals an exercise break with loud music and a trainer's voice. Instead of exercising, the women pull out their drawers, jingling with cups and spoons. The communal sugar rustles. Sandwiches and salads appear from the bags. Hungry Luda loudly pops open a jar of horseradish.

Angela's neighbor at the next desk leans over and shows her something under the desk top. Angela immediately grabs the thing, raises it higher, turns it around, and scrutinizes it with admiration. It is a beautiful imported push-up bra. All the women gaze at the luxurious piece.

"What size is it?" Zena's amazed. "Who can wear something this tiny?"

"Our Angela is as flat as a board with two nipples," snaps fat Luda and all the women are laughing, satisfied.

"Angela, go ahead, try it on!" encourages her friend.

Without a second thought Angela strips to the waist and turns in different directions demonstrating her "two nipples" in front of the open-mouthed old cows. Then, with elegant movements, she puts on the novelty. It fits perfectly. Angela looks so pretty in this unexpected outfit, that all freeze for a second. Then two heads sharply turn—one to the door of the room, another to the boss's door.

But while the first door remains closed, the second one yields Erena, who appears with her straight back and her perfect hair, and glares with her enormous gray eyes at the troublemaker. She asks with a quiet smile.

"Angela, what's this supposed to be?"

Having lost her courage only for a moment, Angela gathers herself and answers, unembarrassed.

"I've tried on a bra. What, is it illegal? It is an exercise break now, anyway."

Feeling that this is not enough, insolent Angela unfastens the bra, takes it off, and places it on the desk in front of her. She then asks her neighbor in a thoughtful voice.

"So what do you suggest, should I buy it? Or shouldn't I?"

The silence in the room turns sepulchral. Erena approaches Angela's desk with an ironic grin.

"You'll go far."

"Oh no, boss," Angela answers in despair. "I'll never manage to get as far as you."

Some co-workers gesture unwillingly at this unprecedented remark.

"What happened, ladies?" Erena turns around. "The exercise break is over. Where is your Communist enthusiasm? Get back to work."

Looking over the heads of her shocked subordinates, she leaves the department.

Shortly after the young girls dash out one by one heading to the ladies room, and leaving the veterans without an opportunity to express their thoughts.

The girls socialize in the bathroom, holding their coffee cups and throwing cigarette butts in the toilet.

After discussing the latest events in the Department with giggles and chokes of laughter Angela says dreamily, "Hey, girls, isn't our Erena as cool as a cucumber. That's the way to be!"

While waiting for the lunch break bell, the women pull their big shopping bags from under the desks and renew their lipstick getting ready to run to the stores.

"So she," continues one of them, having been interrupted mid-word, "took out that padding from her high hairdo. Then she took off her thermal underwear, discreetly, of course, and hid it. Then he attempted to unhook her bra, but all her business trip money was in it, so she started screaming! Afterwards she told us. 'How could he know that the money was in there?' We told her. 'You fool, he wasn't after your money, he was after your breasts!'"

All the women laugh.

"And who remembers that hilarious story about Svetlana?" another storyteller is popping in. "How she decided to follow her Peter-cheater? He told her he was going to visit his brother after work. She knew he was lying. She hurried after him and forgot to put her thermal underwear back on. The temperature outside was minus twenty that day, and she was just in her nylon bikini and pantyhose. She froze everything down there!"

"Look," in a low voice, a young woman with a thick wedding ring on her finger asks another one, without a ring. "When you have orgasms, how is it? What is it, actually? What do you feel?"

The lunch break bell does not allow her to get an answer. All the women spring up from their seats and escape.

3

Erena's grandpa stands on his balcony and enjoys the view of the quiet fall sunset and of his shiny bronze bust in the park. A blissful silence hangs in the air. Only fallen leaves rustle in the park alleys. Grandpa hears the voices of visitors downstairs: Erena's family has just shown up. Vasiliy Vasilich returns to his room.

"You are free now. Go to your husband," he says to Valya who is casually resting on the bed in her usual black net stockings, leafing idly through the *Pravda*.

Valya puts on her white uniform, fixes her blond locks, and withdraws from the office.

Grandpa slowly heads to the living room opulently decorated with Oriental rugs. Erena and Alexei are already sitting in the maroon leather armchairs. Adorable Lucy flies from Mommy to Daddy. Even her brown school uniform looks too cute on the doll-like child.

After mutual greetings, Erena starts talking business:

"Grandpa, Alexei is being pushed out by comrade Kucheroff. The guy definitely knows something. He got the position in less than a week after his initiation. Someone is pushing him up. One of those 'new leaders,' mind you. Alexei is being sent to the East, not to the West. It's a demotion, obviously. Some changes are coming. Some unpleasant changes."

Erena seems to worry more than her husband does. He grins calmly, playing with a lighter.

"Don't fret," he says. "What can they actually do? What can really change here? They'll just make a big fuss as usual and then leave everything as it is. Am I right, Vasiliy Vasilich?"

Grandpa shakes his head hesitatingly.

"I am not so sure," he pronounces rather slowly. "They say the Master is not well. God forbid if the worst happens—we will all be gone. And not abroad, believe me. Everything will be taken from us then: our positions, our homes, cars. And you'll be thankful then that it's not Stalin's rule any more. Back then, the owner's life would be void along with the estate, you know. On the other hand, what can really change? You are a young man, Alexei. These are your first steps in the Central Committee. Wherever you are going to be sent—anything's fair enough. East or West, working abroad is better anyway, than here 'in jail'...You know this, don't you? When you come back, the position will be yours again. While I'm alive...Besides, what is Kucheroff anyway? The son of a maid. He can't rise over his own roost."

The group laughs casually and, obeying the soundless appearance of the maid at the door, moves to the dining room where the table is set modestly but with great taste.

The peaceful meal of the grandfather and the grandchildren is disturbed only by the clink of the silverware and a few comments from Erena.

"Lucy, sweetheart, don't shake your legs under the table. Take the knife in your right hand, dear."

An invisible source produces soft music and the whole group is bathed in the bright rays of sunset, shining through the wide windows. The mansion gradually immerses in bluish twilight...

4

On a murky fall day, the cold rain has just stopped. Early dusk falls on the city. Trolley buses and streetcars, filled to capacity, are carrying home workmen after another long day. The trolley doors, unable to close, are jammed with coats and bags.

From the marble steps of an enormous official building, the higher creatures, members of the Communist Party Central Committee, descend toward the world of commons. They dive into their long black automobiles, which take them, one by one, away from the place of their public service.

Among others, Alexei leaves the building easily running down the stairs. He looks very handsome in his official overcoat and conservative hat. Approaching the expecting car, he suddenly sees a slim girl's figure popping out from around the corner right toward him. Backing away in surprise, Alexei looks at the cute girl with growing interest. She is obviously very young, with bright make-up, and dressed in white pantyhose and high heels in spite of the autumn slush. Her stylish overcoat, with a fur collar and cuffs, is unfastened. Shaking her long hair, the girl steps forward.

"Alexei," not a bit embarrassed she starts, "I work for your wife, Erena, in her department. Yeah...she's at home sick, as you know...and I...I would like to pass some papers to her. Here is some urgent work that she asked me to do. So, could you please do it for me?"

She turns to her purse which hangs on her shoulder, and hardly believing his own eyes, Alexei sees that under her open overcoat she is wearing only these transparent white pantyhose and a white lace push-up bra.

Trying to figure it out, Alexei promptly looks around and approaches the girl.

"What's your name?" he asks.

"Angela," smiles the beauty.

"Well, well, take a seat," Alexei commands, flinging open the car's back door. Making sure that no one can see them, he dives into the car after her.

5

A Monday morning, gray and cloudy, finds the Petrick family at their abundant meal in the kitchen.

"Valya," her mother commands, "get Kolya some pork. Eat up, my sweetheart. Here, take these cute eggplants. These juicy tomatoes! Would you like another cabbage roll? No? Hey, chew, Valya, chew! Stuff your stomach. For the whole week you'll stay there working hard with no homemade anything. Gene, what's wrong? You can't be full yet. Here, take some cream with that coffee. Chocolates? You don't want any? Don't be silly!"

"Valya," her father intervenes. "What about Vasiliy Vasilich? What is he saying about the situation at the top?"

"Nothing," replies Valya, chewing on her food. "What should he say?"

"We all know that there is trouble, isn't there?"

Valya looks at Kolya. He finishes his coffee and nods to her.

"There is no trouble," he says loudly to the silent Petricks, "The old Master just died all right, but Vasiliy sits firmly. No one can move him. He knows how to deal with anybody. Besides, our guys say that this new Master is rather sick, so…perhaps, he's not the last one in Vasiliy's career. And ours, of course."

"Oh, don't you be so sure," Valya's father shakes his head. "Don't be. All of them sat firmly, quite securely. For fifteen years, no one has moved them. Now, he just started and many are moved from their places way down. If, God forbid, he moves Vasiliy Vasilich…we—mother and I, and Gene, we will stay with our own. We can only be kicked out of this apartment. We'll go back to some communal hole, I guess. But you and Valya, where are you going to go if they take away Vasiliy's home and fire all the staff?"

"You won't lose this apartment," Kolya calms him, rising from the table. "And we, Valya and I, will be safe." Kolya sweetly strokes his wife's shoulder. "Vasiliy says a teakettle cannot be covered with ice. So there."

6

In the park in front of a mansion, the morning stillness is broken only by the occasional crow's scream. Vasiliy Vasilich is doing his morning jog around the empty flower beds and damp granite benches. The bronze bust dimly glows under the pale cold sky.

After a filling breakfast and before he goes to the city, Vasiliy Vasilich pushes a button on his intercom and calls the nurse. Valya appears in the doorway and grants him her big flashy smile. Taking off her nurse uniform, she clambers up on the bed, and unfolds *Pravda*.

"In accordance with the retirement regulations and because of the state of his health," she mumbles, "Plenum has satisfied the request of comrade X to retire from the position…"

Valya drops the paper on the floor, slightly brushing a bald spot on Vasiliy Vasilich's head while he's stroking her bare thighs, and pulls from the coffee table another paper, from yesterday.

"'In accordance with the retirement regulations, comrade Y is released from his position…' well, well. All the same again. Everybody's being laid off. This is boring."

Valya drops this paper on the floor as well.

"Boring to death," mutters Vasiliy Vasilich, throwing Valya her uniform. "You are free now. I'm busy."

Valya leaves.

Valya's husband Kolya and his partner-guard are killing time in the mansion's front lobby. Sprawled out in the armchair, Kolya squeezes a matchbox in his strong fingers, rolling it up and down his palm. Muscles on his arm bulge impressively. Valya sits on his lap.

"Vasiliy is so mad," she whispers. "Kolya, it's time to get busy. Find out among yours what's happening? The end of the world?"

"Don't fret," replies Kolya, rolling his wife's fair locks around his hand. You and me, Valya, we'll never fall. We are infallible. Got it? Now get lost, don't keep me from working."

With a light kiss on his cheek, Valya disappears.

Kolya briefly talks to his partner. He points to the telephone, to the clock, then hurriedly leaves the mansion. He hails a chauffeur, who is always ready, sitting in the car, and rides away.

7

In the depth of his enormous, auditorium-like office, Erena's husband looks smaller, despite his height and substantial size. He sits behind the T-shaped desk, surrounded with armchairs for visitors and meetings. He has slid down in his armchair, and is half-lying, with his tie askew, his eyes rolled-up, and his mouth open. He is breathing heavily. His white shirt is bunched up on his chest. It looks like he's not well…Shortly, an expression of bliss spreads over his face accompanied by a groan. In a moment, a marvelous apparition emerges from under the desk. Blushing and slightly disheveled Angela, panting, hurriedly refastens her blouse.

Alexei takes care of himself, tucking his shirt back into his pants. She picks up her pink angora sweater from the floor.

"So, what are you going to tell Erena?" Alexei asks in a husky voice. "You're pretty late."

"I tell her that…I was at the dentist, for an emergency," smiles Angela.

"No, after a dental emergency your breath should smell like medication. She won't believe you."

"Then I'll tell her that I had an emergency gynecologist appointment. A sharp pain in the ovaries."

"Oh, that's better," laughs Alexei loudly. "Exactly, in the ovaries." He rises, buttons his fly, and happy with the whole affair, walks Angela to the door. "Today I have a meeting with the Frenchmen, the perfumers. I'll grab some samples for you. I'll call."

He pinches her behind good-bye.

Standing on her toes, Angela tenderly kisses his closely shaven cheek and, smiling, departs from the top office.

8

A full moon peers into Vasiliy Vasilich's bedroom window. The noble old man sleeps peacefully, robed in his silk pajamas, under the satin down-filled blanket, slightly tossed aside due to the heat. The night is perfectly silent, as it can be only in the suburbs. Suddenly the silence is disrupted by the sound of an approaching vehicle. The gates open quietly, and after a brief pause, a strange noise is heard under the window. Some heavy machinery arrives in the park with the bronze bust. One can hear car doors slamming, and an undertone of male voices.

The moonlight is overshadowed by some other, brighter illumination—a spotlight, powerful enough to break the deep sleep of the mansion owner. Vasiliy Vasilich opens his eyes, raises his head, but sleep overcomes him, and he falls back on the pillow. Meanwhile the noise outside changes its nature. Now one can hear an even grinding of sawing metal, and the short phrases of working people, clear in the quiet frosty air.

"Go ahead. Saw. He's empty inside. Drop your cigarette. You'll take a smoking break after."

"It's hard, goddamit! Who is he, by the way?"

"Oh, shut up. Just do your job and go."

"He's one of those Central Committee big cheeses, freshly demoted, that's all."

"Who cares? You saw, I weld, we're done. Fine with me."

"Guys! Kolya! You'd better close the gates. Why the hell keep them open? Some scum could be loitering around…"

The sound of the saw over metal suddenly stops and a man's voice exclaims.

"See, told ya! He's empty inside, a dummy! Saw, saw! We'll be done shortly. I'm not going to spend all night here."

"Hey, Kolya, get me a rope, there, in my car!"

"Here! Get it up!"

The roar of an engine finally awakens Vasiliy Vasilich. He sits on his bed. Looks of perplexity, suspicion, and fear each cross his face in turn. Throwing off his blanket, he stands barefoot on the shag carpet, and timidly approaches the window. Through the half-opened silk curtains he sees his favorite park, disfigured by the presence of alien subjects: a hoist with a hook and a thick rope on it, a junky van, resembling one of the police, and a gray *Volga*. With this particular car, only color alone says clearly that the owner is not a bigwig—they only use black cars—but merely a not-so-important Committee person. So, why do they dare come here? They tie the rope around the hefty bronze forehead of the bust. The other end of the rope is attached to the hook of a hoist. They saw the bronze head off the neck. Following a sign from an invisible someone in the darkness, the head moves away from the bust and flies up, then down, where the four workmen catch it on a tarp stretched in their hands. They wrap it up and place it into the van. At their feet Vasiliy Vasilich, hardly believing his own eyes, sees another head, taken from the van, with the same solid hairdo, but with someone else's face which he is not able to recognize from a distance. They tie the same rope around the new head, and it goes up, then down, landing under the cheerful exclamations of the workmen, directly onto the cut neck of the bust. The man with the saw on the high ladder is replaced with a welder. Bright sparks pierce the air, and the new head is firmly installed on the bust. Lights reflect in the unnaturally widened eyes of Vasiliy Vasilich.

"That's it. This is the end. Demoted, robbed, stripped." Short and sharp thoughts claw his mind. "They didn't even bother to let me know first. Just sent this trash to chalk me out. Tomorrow in the papers…After all these years…"

He turns like a sleepwalker on stiff legs. He passes his bed, his office, steps on the carpeted stairs, but suddenly is startled by another picture. Before him shines a white marble stairway lit with a million lights stretching upward and covered with a red carpet. He hears noise growing louder in his ears—the noise of applause and cheers. At the very top of the shiny stairway, someone invisible due to the bright light stretches a glowing golden star to Vasiliy Vasilich. On the rough, hairy hand, which carries the star, he sees an ugly prison tattoo. Vasiliy Vasilich, extremely puzzled, turns his eyes to the people surrounding the Master. He sees thieves' repulsive mugs with rotten teeth over the snow-white shirts and black ties of the Central Committee leaders. They all stare at him with their gloomy criminal eyes. At this moment, the golden star, his dear award, thrusts into his chest, as sharp as a drill.

"Uh," he exclaims briefly, loosing his breath, and rolls down the stairs with a crash.

9

The workday at the Department of Information is in full swing, and the lunch break is coming soon. Coffee is finished, all neighboring departments have been visited, some women are still chewing on something, and the others are getting their shopping bags ready for their daily march through the stores.

"Girls, do you remember that 'babe' I showed you in the morning? She stopped by to pick up a brochure, remember?" loudly asks Angela, who still reigns in the "youth" corner. Her long hair is fashionably cropped in front, and sticks out over her forehead in different directions. It gives an impression of a woman just out of bed after wild embraces. The tips of her hair are bleached, almost colorless. She is wearing a stylish stonewashed denim skirt. Her crimson blouse is of the season's newest wrinkled silk. Under her skirt, there is a pair of black lace pantyhose. While she is talking, women are studying her new outfit with their eyes wide-open. Some of them even approach her to get a closer look.

Some girls remember that "babe" who stopped by in the morning.

"So that's her!" victoriously exclaims Angela. "Am I right, Lud?" she asks the miserable fat woman, who is just finishing chewing her pound of lard on rye. Luda looks at Angela with sheer hate.

"Hey, Lud, that's her, right? Lud, tell them!"

"First off, I am not 'Lud' to you!" Luda retorts in outrage. "And second, you should respect me and call me by my full name!"

"You mean *your* full name? You mean respect *you*?" Angela becomes insolent. "You mean I *should*? Look, sweetie, tuck up your boobs or you're gonna trip over them!"

The fat woman leaps up to her feet. Department veterans are speechless. Young girls giggle. Trying to change the subject, one of the women timidly continues the topic started by Angela.

"It was Lisa Organ, who was here this morning. And she is the one, who got 'the letter.'"

"Is that her last name or her nickname?" asks one of the younger women.

"Of course it's her last name," more confidently answers the story-teller, trying to steer off the episode with Luda faster. "She, you know…if you want to hear her story, I can tell," she turns to the girls.

"But of course," they laugh. Angela studies herself in the mirror on her desk. She opens her new French cosmetic set under envious glances.

"So, for your information, Lisa Organ was a rare whore," contin-ues the storyteller. "I mean, that kind of whore that smokes and burns! She told us everything herself. She could do it on the train, on the platform, on all her business trips, at all the collective farms where we were harvesting potatoes, wherever! Once it was with the whole soccer team. Or, maybe, she was lying. Maybe not the whole team."

"So, so!" her listeners hurry her up. "With the whole soccer team, or a part of it, what's the difference?"

"Big difference," sticks in someone from the far corner. "The whole team means twenty two members, or how many—eleven? And a part could mean just one, which is nothing awesome. Look, isn't she a labor heroine?"

"Oh, I think you'll find that even twenty two may not be enough," shouts another woman from a different corner.

"I don't mind, actually," follows the answer, "I have nothing to lose. My husband warned me when we were young, don't rush, don't spend everything at once, nothing would be left for later. But I was young, hot and slim, just like our Angela, I wanted more and more! So, now nothing left, as he predicted!"

"Okay, let's finish with Organ," shouts one of the girls. All the women laugh.

"Oh really? Everyone who could, has already finished with her!"

The story continues.

"So, once on a business trip Lisa met a guy who was not the one-night-stand type, he was a solid one. I mean he wanted more. It happened in Crimea."

"You mean, he wanted to come here from Crimea just to screw her?" innocently asks Angela.

"Maybe. Don't interrupt me. He wrote her a letter, but sent it here, to the company address. She got the letter, read it, put it in her drawer, and went to the bathroom. On her way back, she saw that all the guys, who were smoking in the corridor, were looking at her, laughing. Not understanding a thing, she goes to her department. And guess what? Her boss, the pig, has taken the letter from her drawer and he has read it aloud. And in the letter there were words like, 'Lisa, your breasts are like two white swans!'"

Everybody laughs.

"So now they call her 'swan breasts' from that day on. And that's her real nickname. And her boobs are really huge, you know."

"Did she say anything to her boss, the pig?"

"She did, but he told her, 'Unrelated subjects at your work place. I'll bring it to Personnel.' She had nothing to do but shut up. Her lover came here later and he called her from the downstairs. Her boss picked up the phone, and said, 'Who you want? Organ? She ain't here. I don't know nothing and I doesn't care if you wait or not. You ain't the only one who wants Organ here.' He was a real jerk, never spoke correctly."

Everybody giggles. The door is flung open and in flies Zena, the typist.

"Girls, Erena isn't here?" she shouts from the threshold.

"No," they answer. "Why are you screaming? You think she doesn't know that you are always late?"

"Oh, no, it's not about that." Zena hurries to sit near her typewriter. "I mean that something's gonna happen."

"What?"

"Old Vasiliy kicked the bucket. Erena's grandfather. That's what. You'll see it in the papers tomorrow, I guess. Or maybe the day after tomorrow. I overheard it from my neighbors. Remember I told you about them? Valya's parents. They have such a thin wall now in their bathroom. I told you how she ruined our wall, the bitch! So now I place an empty glass jar there, I press my ear to it, and I hear all the federal news from their apartment. They are chatting in the kitchen, same as all of us. So, he died. Erena will be fired now."

"Dream on! Who would dare touch them? Are you nuts?"

"I'm telling you, she'll be fired! She doesn't even have a high school diploma!"

"So what? It's like trying to scare a porcupine with a bare ass! Which one of our bosses has any diplomas, for God's sake!"

"Oh, they do. Not worth the paper they are printed on, but they still have some diplomas."

"So, they'll draw one for Erena. Big deal! She's the boss and you are the fool! When you're the boss, then she'll be the fool. Now sit quietly and don't talk too much. Or some kind soul will report you."

Amidst the noise, the lunch break bell sounds, and all the women run away from their work places.

10

Lit by a green table lamp, a small family conference is taking place in Erena's living room. Her father sits in an armchair, hidden behind a newspaper. His son-in-law nervously walks back and forth. Erena's mother, on the sofa, weeps, biting her handkerchief. Erena feeds her daughter Lucy orange slices near the coffee table.

"Okay," pronounces Erena's father, throwing down the paper. "It'll end somehow."

"How? How will it end?" his son-in-law shouts in rage, approaching the older man with his fists clenched. "Do you understand that a department like mine cannot be merely 'cancelled through reorganization,' and if it can, then I, *I* should be safe. I should be moved to the same position level in a different department! Now I am just kicked out, 'in accordance with the department cancellation!' What's this supposed to mean? What should I do now? Sit here, in this jail of a country till the end of time?" Suddenly he turns to Erena. "See, I told you, I should have accepted that first offer, I should have gone that time, to the East, wherever! There, abroad, they can't get rid of people this fast. It takes time to sweep away all the folks here first. If I had gone, Kucheroff would be the loser now!"

"Oh, don't worry, Kucheroff wouldn't lose! He doesn't have a grandfather who died. He's a bum. Bastards like him sit tighter and keep longer. If they start, they never stop!" replies Erena, more aggressively than usual.

"Don't you understand that Papa is gone?" starts Erena's mother hysterically, swaying with her enormous bosom. "Don't you realize that we are on our own now?" she addresses her numb husband.

"That now we are forced to save every...hundred! We don't know what's gonna happen to us in this hellhole. Enemies surround us! 'To our regret we inform.' They 'regret,' they 'inform,' those scoundrels, scum, and trash! I know their regrets. They never appreciated Papa, they never listened to him. He always said it was not right to criticize ex-masters and their deeds. He said never flirt with the masses. Never give them any doubt in their leaders, dead or alive. The masses are angry, mad. Just let them think that one of us can be wrong and they think we all are. He said that the teakettle has to be on the fire. If they don't fear us, then they want us to fear them. Wasn't he right? Always, always right. But wait, now they started these stupid reforms. They are undermining themselves. Just read the papers! Those scribblers have gotten to our privileges. They are allowed now! Everything that was special, our own, exclusive, is shut down, our special stores, farms, resorts. They've written out everything! Everything that belonged to us for decades. People never had an idea, so it never bothered them. Now they are giving them ideas. Look at those titles! 'Golden vegetables,' 'Privileged consumers,' 'Who pays for the pure products,' 'Selected places for selected people,' just look at this! What are we supposed to eat or drink now? That communal dirt for the masses? How are we supposed to survive?"

"And the house," the son-in-law interjects, "Grandpa's house? Didn't you hear? They're turning it into children's sanatorium! And what are they going to do with our apartments? Are they taking them away too?"

"They won't take them away," replies Erena's father. "There is influence at the top that can leave them to the current residents, but with a regular Residential-Exploitation Management."

"What?" jumps up his son-in-law. "Do you have the slightest idea what that regular management is?"

"What about you? Do you know?" asks his father-in-law ironically.

"I don't. And I don't want to know. I can guess—no hot water for months; no heat in winter; leaking roofs and sinks; roaches, mice, rats! You can read it in the paper in the *Letters* column. I don't want to stay in this jail! Do you understand? The end! The end! This is the end of the world!" Alexei walks up to the wall and desperately beats the Oriental rug on it with his fists.

"Stop being hysterical," Erena looks at him scornfully. "In front of the child! Nothing's gonna happen to us. We'll work. We'll be useful."

"You mean, *you*, and work?" Alexei attacks Erena now. "Didn't you show your best working abilities at your 'women-only-department-of-gossip-and-chitchat?' You'd better go finish high school first! You had just enough education to get pregnant at school!"

Father, Mother and Erena simultaneously stand up from their seats. Understanding that he has gone too far, Alexei backs up to the dark corner of the living room.

Ice glitters in Erena's eyes. With a regal gesture, she points to the door and quietly pronounces.

"Get out, now. You son of a bitch."

Lucy looks at her mommy with great adoration.

Trying to fix the situation, Alexei babbles.

"Erena, I'm sorry, I'm sorry. I didn't mean it." He throws himself at her feet, catches her hand, and kisses it. His voice trembles.

"Forgive me, Erena. I've lost my mind. I've gone crazy. Please, don't be angry."

Erena silently sits back in the armchair.

Her mother and father, exchanging glances, take their seats also. In the silence Erena says quietly, but firmly, "There is no need to go crazy. Aren't you ashamed? Grandpa has not been buried yet. That is what we must be thinking about, everything else later."

She cleans her hands with a tissue, placing the last slice of orange into Lucy's mouth, and heads toward the door, commanding the others: "Let's go."

11

Among the dreary landscape of the city dump a flock of crows dash around with loud cries. Some ghostly figures dig in the piles of garbage, and the dump workers in their enormous gloves loiter in the twilight.

A long black automobile quietly approaches. Two of the workers rush toward it. Lead by Erena, the noble family, instinctively shaking off something invisible, leaves the car and lines up alongside, not daring to step forward. They wrinkle their noses in disgust.

"How are you?" Erena greets the workers. "I hope everything's all right? Where is Grandpa?"

They vigorously nod at her words, and disappear for awhile, then drag out a heavy bronze head, so tragically cut out from the bust of the unforgettable Vasiliy Vasilich.

The head goes into the car trunk. Erena, graciously counts out some bank notes, not taking off her delicate gloves. She then turns and pulls from the car two bottles of vodka. She hands them to the workers. They grab the gift with trembling hands.

"And please, forget you ever saw us," she suggests, smiling graciously.

They only nod, their mouths stretched to their ears in an ingratiating smile. The black automobile disappears.

Fresh Wind of Perestroika

1

On a gloomy Sunday morning, Zena, with a set of rollers in her hair, is lying in her warm nightgown with her arms and legs outstretched under the thick wadded blanket. She feels stuffy. Her half-awakened, balding husband unconsciously feels her hips under the blanket with his sleepy fingers. Soon the spouses turn to the same side and indulge in sluggish lovemaking, partly falling asleep, partly continuing their affair, when the more energetic Zena pushes her sleepy husband with her elbow. All of a sudden a loud voice, amplified with a megaphone, is heard from outside. The voice approaches and sounds under the windows. Very close, perhaps, from the park nearby comes the hum of a big crowd, exclamations, and fragments of conversations. The megaphone sounds again. A familiar female voice is preaching outside.

"Our Communist party urges us to start perestroika, to reconstruct our party, to rebuild our society, and to decline all the party privileges voluntarily. The party's property must pass back to the people. Great Lenin's modesty, having been perverted through the years of stagnation by our former stagnating leaders, should now triumph again. For this purpose, our party started perestroika! We must all join and support!"

Zena and her husband, finally fully awake, run to the window. They see a crowd in the park. "Long live perestroika!" "Down with bureaucracy!" "1986 is the year of Great Perestroika—our new era!" the slogans say. On the park bench stands their neighbor Valya, with her shiny blond locks, in her dark mink coat. She waves her hand, sending into the air bright reflective diamond rays.

"Now my friend Angela, a simple working class representative from one of our city plants, will read you her poem about the bureaucrats. About those who have insulted us, the workers, for many long years, and who now, under the fresh wind of perestroika, should be banished from our lives forever!"

Valya jumps down from the bench, and takes from her husband Kolya's hand an official folder with a KGB note on it "Poet Cohen's trial. 1979. Sentenced to exile." She pulls out of the folder a hand-written piece of paper, and gives it to Angela. The "simple working class representative" is dressed in shiny black vinyl pants. While a hushed crowd studies the amazing pants, Angela reads the poem in her loud expressive voice.

A FAMILY

Your father looks so young, he's thin and
tanned.
Your mom is fresh, well rested, underweight.
She looks not like a mom, but like a friend.
And you, yourself, you've got all their skill—
To tame, to honor, and if not, to kill.
Your husband's from a family like yours—
He is so wealthy, though not that bright,
His car is top, his clothes designed.
And he's attached to you with all his might.
Your house is huge, but you do not have friends,
Besides, the voices irritate your dog,
Among the things, that matter, and that don't,
You pick up so infallibly, all brands.
How do the miserable people live?
It's not your problem, lucky wealthy girl.
You take it all for granted, after all!
...But I remember, we've been taught in class
That bourgeoisie does not exist as a class.

The crowd applauds furiously.

2

A strong wind tears the last leaves off the trees on a dark November evening. In the light of the scarce street lamps, a well-groomed woman with a remarkable bosom hurries somewhere. On a quiet curved street, Erena's mother stops in front of a tall old building, quickly looks around, and slips inside.

She goes up a dark dilapidated stairway to the top floor. Cats spring from under her feet. The landing of the staircase is stuffed with crates full of potatoes, saved for the coming winter. A dirty door is covered in graffiti. The elegant woman, obviously not used to such places, rings the doorbell. The door opens. There is darkness behind it, and only some trembling light is visible inside. A soft singing is heard from the depths of the apartment.

Someone invisible in the dark leads her by the hand to the far room. She mechanically throws down her coat, not minding where it falls. She pulls off her kid gloves and her expensive leather boots. With a quick movement of her hand, she loosens her hair. Now she looks like everyone else in the room, which is full of longhaired bare-foot women in their shapeless baggy dresses, and shaven-headed men, decorated with wooden beads. The majority of them sit on the floor, crossing their bare feet, some of them rock slightly in an improvised dance, raising their bare arms high. On the low table, around which the people have taken their seats, black candles burn dimly. A plaintive song sounds louder. "Hare Rama, Hare Krishna, Hare Krishna, Hare Rama, Hare Rama, Hare Rama, Hare Rama, Rama, Rama, Rama…"

Erena's mother joins the others. Rocking from side to side, she starts babbling the prayer song along with them.

After a while a very skinny man with thick round glasses and a goatee stands up near the table. He starts the "seance." He stretches his arms over his congregation. All the people freeze in reverence. Only two quick and noiseless women finish their preparations for the sacred meal. On the table, between the candles, they put out dishes with rice, dried fruit and curled dry carrots. In front of Erena's mother appears a pile of raw beans. This is a ritual dish as well.

"Brothers and sisters," the guru starts preaching, "let the power of Cosmos, the Great Count Shakya Moony, and the undamaged aura of our own goodness keep us safe. Hare Rama, Hare Krishna!"

"Hare Rama, Hare Krishna," the crowd repeats.

"Remember, my children, nothing in this world happens without a reason, every phenomenon, every action has their beginning in the Cosmos, in the Absolute. Our karma is bigger than our life. Fulfill your karma and you'll be safe. If not in this world, so in the Cosmos. Hare Rama, Hare Krishna."

"Hare Rama, Hare Krishna," everybody babbles.

"Put your bare feet on the ground. Pour a bucket of icy cold water over your head. All the cosmic energy will be yours. Nothing bad will ever happen to a good person, and only Great Russia will stop the invasion of the black devils into Europe and all the other continents. Shambala is benevolent to us. Expect the great last opposition of good and evil. Hare Rama, Hare Krishna!"

"Hare Rama, Hare Krishna!"

"The Himalayas have sent their cosmic energy to Russia, and I am a messenger of these cosmic powers. Listen brothers and sisters, the length of my aura reaches twenty-five meters. Anyone, whose aura is black, has nothing to do among us. I pour on you three bowls of pure cosmic energy! Hare Rama! Hare Krishna!"

"Hare Rama, Hare Krishna!"

"Hindi-Russi bhai, bhai!"

"Bhai, bhai!"

"Sister Lakshmi, repeat today's theme, inspired by Buddha!"

A woman with a disheveled librarian look, sitting next to Erena's mother, stands up, extinguishing a candle with the edge of her dress, and jabbers, "Nothing happens without a reason. All the phenomena have their beginning in the Cosmos."

The extinguished candle smokes thinly. Erena's mother inhales this smoke and unwillingly produces a deafening sneeze. The sharp sound of the breaking fastener on her bra accompanies this sneeze. Her enormous, luxurious breasts, not restrained by anything any more, flop directly onto the raw bean plate, from which the largest bean flies out, heading for the eye of the inspired preacher. Thick glasses save the guru's eye. He exclaims joyfully.

"Rejoice, brothers and sisters! Under the power of our prayer sister Mahajana broke free from her shackles!"

3

In the spacious building of the International Airport, crowds of people ply back and forth. Kolya on duty hides behind a potted rhododendron, which stands at the edge of a fountain. A young policeman with a bright blush on his cheeks—proof of a recent farmer past—approaches, and ducking under the lush plant, salutes.

"Allow me to speak, comrade major of the KGB," he whispers.

"What do you want?" furiously whispers Kolya.

"They've announced an arrival from Paris. Oh, sorry, I mean they've announced a departure to Paris. And *they* are not here yet. Maybe, they got wind of it?"

"Go, Stezenko. Go to your place," Kolya shoos him away. "They will be here any moment. Stay there and wait for my signal. Get lost!"

The policeman rapidly runs away.

A line of black *Volgas* rolls to the airport. One by one police officers of high rank emerge from them, take off their service caps, and wipe perspiration from their foreheads. They crack jokes and chuckle. Then, led by the General, they head to the airport building. After them, porters roll carriages with empty suitcases, ready for shopping abroad.

Waiting for an airport shuttle, the high-ranking police officers say good-bye to their younger comrades. The General, who has suddenly decided to land in Paris with a European look, energetically takes off his uniform coat and puts on a black smoking jacket. Chuckling good-naturedly, he addresses the young man standing close by, red-faced from tension.

"Okay, Stezenko, do your duty here. We are off to Paris. We'll attend an Interpol conference and be back soon." The General pulls out a small box from his pocket, takes a golden signet ring and struggles to put it on his sausage-like finger.

"How do I look? Like a European? Are we going to rock Paris, or not?" he makes a move to hug the soldier.

"Don't touch me," hysterically squeals Stezenko, "you aren't going to Paris, you shameful corrupted old-timers! Now is *our time*—perestroika!" The valiant KGB major Kolya rushes in with his men, who appear from all four sides, toward the trapped officers. The arrests begin. Confused high-ranked officers turn around, unable to comprehend what is happening. The arresting team, armed and with cuffs ready, surrounds them in a tight ring. Kolya steps ahead.

"Comrades," he shouts to the crowd, squeezing *Pravda* in his hand and chopping the air with it. "You are present at the capture of a group of corrupt high-ranking police officers, who have abused their power and their people's trust for years. These bribers and molesters will be taken to court, where their guilt will be proven. Now instead of Paris we will send them to the isolation ward! Long live perestroika, comrades!"

Canary police cars appear with flashing lights, and Kolya's men load them with corrupt officials, accompanied by the roar of the departing *Air-France* plane.

4

The Musical Center made of glass and cement, glows under the winter sun. Occasional flurries fly by. A long black car brings an elegant man in a brown suede coat to the "Employees Only" entrance. He hurries inside, holding the edges of his white scarf. He greets the cleaning ladies, and the girls from Administration, runs through the backstage, takes off his coat somewhere on his way, and appears in the auditorium, flattening his dark blonde locks with his palms. Confidently he takes his place behind the directors stand, gives a command, "We can start now," to someone invisible, and pulls a table lamp closer. Valya's brother, Gene, is now the head of the well-known Musical Center.

There is a little anxiety backstage. One of the administrative girls hisses with her painted mouth. "Don't you understand? Gene himself will listen to you. Stop messing around, divide by bands!"

The audition starts. Gene asks all of them the same question. "So, what do you have?" Some of the musicians give Gene blank envelopes along with their lyric sheets. They suspiciously resemble bribe envelopes, well remembered from the "stagnant past." Gene tucks them under the stand without a second glance. He suggests to some female singers, "Call me at home tonight, the outcome of your audition is not clear yet."

One of the bands goes for the folk style, with a drawn-out melody and loud drums.

> "Let them like it or not,
> Russian beauty will rise,
> And the bells will ring loudly!"

Looking in the text of the lyrics, Gene irritably interrupts:

"No, no! You should at least make some sense! Redo it like this, perhaps.

> "If the Russian beauty
> Won't be liked by them,
> Then the bells will ring!"

5

Erena Novikova in her black mink coat passes the gates of "eternal peace." The silence of the cemetery is disturbed only by the wind, which rustles in the bare limbs of the tall, gloomy trees. The tombstones are covered with a thin layer of snow. Here and there, one can see withered chrysanthemums. She approaches the cemetery shop and sharply pushes the door. A big man dressed in a worn army coat almost falls on her from the inside.

"Oh," he mumbles, "I was about to leave, and here's a lady!" he stretches his arms widely, obviously drunk. "Are you looking for me, Madam?"

"Perhaps, for you," says Erena, taking his huge paw off her bosom. The man looks at his hand in surprise, as if it had just landed on Erena's breast on its own. "I need a sculptor, are you the one?"

"Oh, Madam, for you, always," he babbles, trying to stay vertical. "Do you desire a tombstone?"

"Yes. Actually, I only need a pedestal. I have a head."

"You have a head? Uh-huh, you do, absolutely. I guess, you are very grief stricken, Madam?" asks the sculptor, gazing at her suspiciously. Erena looks at him with her lucid eyes, slightly raising an eyebrow.

"Oh, sorry," he interrupts himself. "For whom do you need a tombstone, dare I ask? For your husband?"

"No, for my grandfather."

"Don't you need one for your husband, anyway?" the sculptor unsteadily backs up to the shop. Erena follows him. Among the marble and granite blocks standing here and there, she notices a weird construction—a truncated pyramid made of black and white marble blocks.

"How about this one?" she asks, pointing with her gloved hand to the construction.

"Oh, Madam, this is not a tombstone. This is, so to speak, a sculpture, a piece of art. I do not have a studio, as you can see, so I'm forced to create my art works right here in the shop. Along with the main manufacturing, so to speak."

"Oh please, what kind of sculpture is this? It's just a tombstone, and it looks like exactly the one I need."

"This *is* a sculpture, Madam," insists its creator. "It's called *Apotheosis of Communism.*"

"Very appropriate," agrees Erena. "I want to take it for my grandpa's grave. How much?"

"A simple tombstone is merely five hundred, but this is a sculpture, a work of art…"

"Okay, how much?"

"Five hundred and ten. Only ten—right now," hurriedly agrees the creator. Erena pulls out a sparkling bottle of vodka from her handbag, and having accepted it on his outstretched fingers, the man backs to the far corner.

"So tomorrow we'll install it. The ground on the grave is set by now." Erena is heading to the door. "The money comes after installation," she adds, leaving the shop.

6

Erena, Alexei, and Lucy are standing in front of the tombstone of the unforgettable Vasiliy Vasilich. At their feet is a pile of suitcases and traveling bags. There is no one else around. The new monument is luxurious and original. The black and white marble pyramid is crowned with the bronze head of the old man. At the foot of it there is a fresh bunch of yellow mums. A black veil hangs from Erena's hat, shading her eyes. Erena crumples a handkerchief in her hand. Alexei is bored, Lucy jumps up and down to stay warm.

"That's it, let's go," finally says Erena with a sigh. Alexei takes the suitcases. Lucy puts on her little backpack.

They head to the suburban railway station. After a long ride in the cold and empty suburban train, they appear at a well-known location, the former residence of Erena's grandpa. One can hardly recognize it now. The bronze bust with the head of the latest people's leader is surrounded by rusted and broken children's swings. Stray dogs are digging in a sandbox. On the facade of the mansion, there are damp spots with peeling plaster. Cheap rags hang in the windows instead of designer drapery. The family timidly approaches the house. A huge trash container is overloaded with garbage, towering twice as high as the container itself. Garbage covers the ground all around.

With horror, they enter under the gaily-painted sign "Children's Sanatorium 'Winnie the Pooh,'" and appear in the vestibule decorated with withered potted plants on the windowsills, and healthcare posters pinned to the walls. The vestibule is now divided into cubicles with cardboard walls and doors to offices. On one of them there is a sign "Head of the Sanatorium. Dr. Petrick." Feeling confused, Erena pushes the door open. Behind the desk, a busy blond woman counts something with a help of calculator and writes the results in a thick notebook. She raises her head. Her eyes joyfully light up.

"Erena," she whispers and stands up to hug her old friend.

"Valya," Erena cannot help her tears and cries like a little girl on the shoulder of her former classmate. "Valya, you won't believe it," babbles Erena, blowing her nose in her handkerchief and wiping away tears. "Our building was given to the General Exploitation Management, you know. And they have such disorder there. We have not had hot water for a week! And the day before yesterday the furnace failed. God only knows when they are gonna fix it. It's impossible to live like that. And, besides, Alexei and I, we both are unemployed. You know his department was terminated. I was forced to quit after they demoted the Minister of Agriculture. I can't,"—she emits a new wave of tears. "I can't see how *they* rule the show. I can't!"

"Oh, don't cry," Valya calms her, "I have a teacher's position open here. It's convenient. You can live right here in the sanatorium. Do you want to? And I'll talk to Kolya. He'll find something for Alexei. Besides, he can take Lucy to school in the mornings. He's riding alone in this huge car to the city and back every day. Oh, don't you cry! I'll arrange everything, Erena. We'll survive! Let's go to the second floor. For now, I can give you just one room. Later we'll clear out a couple of bedrooms. Everything's gonna be fine!"

They go to Grandpa's former bedroom, but there are no wall-to-wall shag carpets, and no silk blankets. There is no marble coffee table or stereo system anymore. *Everything* is gone. Only Grandpa's bed, now covered with a cheap throw, is left. Erena falls on it in her mink, cries and hugs it, as if it is all that's left of her past life, gone forever.

"Tonight, I'm going to sleep over at my mom's place," says Valya, standing nearby. "Make yourself comfortable here. Don't cry Erena. In the children's sanatorium you'll be safe!"

It quickly darkens outside the window. Valya and Kolya say goodbye to Erena's family and withdraw into the long black automobile, winking farewell with its red taillights. Erena, Alexei and Lucy have their supper of canned food in the kitchen.

"I'm cold," whines Lucy. "I want to sleep."

"Okay, sweetheart, let's go," Erena stands up. Together they head to the bedroom on the second floor. Erena places Lucy on the bed, covers her tightly with a blanket, and kisses her good night. "Sleep now, dear." She quietly goes downstairs.

Alexei stands near the radiator with a gloomy look. "Like a corpse's feet," he whispers. Erena touches the radiator. "Yes, it's cold," she agrees and leaves in search of someone to manage the problem. In the former guard's hut, she finds a snoring watchman. He sleeps in his dirty overcoat. Having hardly awakened him, Erena asks, "Why is it so cold?"

The watchman does not look too sober. He barely pronounces the words in his broken language.

"See, the boiler is to fix. Blown up is the boiler, I say. I told madam Valya, but when they to fix boiler, I don't know, my sweet dame. So, go on sleep so far. Children, ya know, will come at spring only. So till spring it can stay unfixed, ya see, boiler, I mean."

Erena returns to Alexei in despair.

"I can't sleep like this," he mumbles, "with cold food in my stomach, and in a cold bed. I at least want some hot tea. The gas is gone, what else is there?"

"A fireplace," pronounces Erena in prostration. "But there is no firewood. There must be kerosene stove in the side pantry. It was always there just in case…of nuclear war…"

"Well, this *is* your nuclear war," Alexei is losing his patience. "Look, Erena, do something. Put the teakettle on the stove."

Her coat over her dress, Erena goes to the dark pantry with a dirty window. There is the small kerosene stove on the table. Erena lights it, places a teakettle on the top, and turns to the window. She presses her beautiful little nose to the cold glass. There, behind the glass, in the blue light of a street lamp, stray cats circle around the garbage container, making funny noises during their quick fights. A bigger cat chases away a smaller one. A mother cat pushes her kitten closer to food. An observer cat sits on the very top of the garbage pile and quietly looks down at the crowd. There is life there, and it goes by at its own pace.

Erena's eyes start to fill with sparkling tears. The glass becomes misty and glows dimly. She abruptly turns back to the stove, and before her very eyes, a teakettle, placed on the fire, is rapidly covering with ice...

THE END

Vofkulak

The woods stood still and silent under a dreary sky. Covered with dry leaves, the dead body blended into the landscape like a fallen tree.

An old man in rags was passing by. He stopped and looked at the body. He tried to pull the goat skin shoes off the cold legs, but they did not let go. He whistled to his little girl, who was picking up brushwood nearby, and they slowly went downhill, home.

At night, the tiny mountain village sank into a gloomy silence. In a poor hut, the little girl was weeping over the old man's dead body. He was brought home from the woods with a deep wound in his neck. She cried herself to sleep. Her little face was marred by a hare-lip, her right hand lacked two fingers.

At dawn two villagers brought a motionless young woman from the woods to her parents' house, and knocked at the door. A deep bleeding wound was on her neck. Her mother ran out of the house, weeping. Her father quietly took an axe from behind the door, and headed to the woods.

❧   ❧   ❧

In daylight, the whole village appeared deserted, morose and silent—no church, no tavern, no playground, and no children—a crammed refuge for the sick and the damned. Their life was about survival. Their days were filled with a primal struggle for every crumb of bread. They bore marks—distorted faces, three-fingered hands, and webbed toes. They were lost forever in the mountain village without roads to the outside world.

Time moved like a pestle, circling, grinding them into dust, repeating the same movements, the same events day by day, hour by hour. Sometimes it moved back. Death came by storm, approached as fast as a wild animal with burning red eyes and countless legs. The gigantic iron wolf ran by the silent homes, dropping bloody foam, leaving deep footprints in the muddy soil, and disappearing into the woods.

❋   ❋   ❋

In the old man's hut the little girl sat on the floor grinding oats in a stone mortar. The old man was working on a goatskin, stretched on a board. A redheaded boy opened the door—the village orphan. He worked in the villagers' houses day after day, for a bowl of flour soup. He did all kinds of work, and heard all kinds of stories. They called him Orphan. He sat next to the old man, and started scraping the goatskin.

"Say, Old Man," he said, "our blacksmith is making iron hooks for the wolf. Do you know that?"

"Yeah," said the old man, "But there is no wolf. There is a werewolf. A 'vofkulak' in the old language. Vofkulak is an old story."

"People forget how to hunt a werewolf," continued Old Man. "I tried to tell them, but they wouldn't listen. Wait, after he kills a dozen, they'll come here, they'll listen. It's not easy hunting a werewolf. You have to know the moves, the words. You have to sacrifice a man to him. That's what makes Vofkulak turn into a human. Only then, you can kill him. You won't catch him in the woods."

"How do you know all that?" Orphan asked, "you haven't even been to the woods lately."

"I don't have to go there to know what's going on. Listen to what people say. He never kills a hare or a goat. He leaves no waste. His footprints are too deep. He's heavier than any animal. He's got many legs, red eyes, and iron hair. What do you think he is?"

❀   ❀   ❀

On the edge of the village, near a bald slope, sat a lonely hut. A long ladder led to the garret. Two brothers and their old mother lived in the hut. The older brother, Carver, was tall and thin, with wild black hair and a pale face. The younger one was a cripple lying on a bench all of his life. He did not speak, but moaned and shook his head.

Carver was climbing down from the garret when a sudden cry flew from the village, "Vofkulak, Vofkulak!" He stopped and turned around. The village was still and silent. He looked the other direction. The woods were still. He made another step down, but slipped and fell into the house through the trap door. He stood up, and rubbed his knee. His mother looked at him and sighed.

He sat down to work. Carving a wooden spoon, he listened to his mother's stories about Vofkulak. "They say Vofkulak hunts people in the woods," she said. "That woman from the third house is still sick. He killed someone, too."

"You don't have to go to the woods today," he said.

"I have to. Tomorrow is our turn to feed Orphan. I have to check the hare trap. They say he can run around as a wolf or as a man. You never know."

"Stay at home," he said. "I'll go to the woods myself."

He wanted to tell her that people were doing more harm to themselves than any beast could do, but before he could speak a stone was thrown into his window. "Vofkulak!" he heard, "Vofkulak!"

❦   ❦   ❦

Next morning Orphan knocked at the smith's door. "Why are you here?" the smith greeted him. "Today is not my turn. You go to the garret hut, don't you?"

"I'd rather work for you," said Orphan. "I don't know if it's true, but people say that Vofkulak lives there."

"Fine, but tomorrow go to them. I can't feed you for two days in a row. Besides, there won't be any work to do. I've made enough iron hooks for the whole village. See, people are coming now to pick them up."

Outside the smith's hut they gathered in a crowd. The smith held the white-hot metal hook with his bare hand while forming it with a hammer, and then tossed it into a bucket that sizzled and smoked.

"You can only kill him with an iron hook," said one of the villagers. "He's got iron skin. Knives just break on it."

"He must be limping today. Last night I caught him by the leg," said another. "He ran away, but I saw his blood. It was black."

"You know you can only catch him by the neck, not by the leg. Now you just made him even madder."

"I'm telling you, he must be lame. We can recognize him now."

"Old Man said we have to feed him a man. Then we can kill him."

"No," said Orphan, handing iron hooks to the villagers, "there is no need to feed him a man. I know. Old Man told me. We should tie the iron hooks to knotted cords. He can only be killed with the iron hook on a knotted cord. That's what he said. And we need soap made of dogs' fat. Old Man said so."

"That's right," agreed someone. "We need a soap made of dogs to attract him. He will follow the smell of his kin."

They went to the woods. Covered with dry leaves, among stubs and shrubs, the dead body looked like a fallen tree. The dead man's hand still clutched an axe.

Orphan worked in the garret hut for the day. The old woman struggled to put together a meal. Her ailing son was sitting on the bench, whispering to himself, spitting and shaking.

"People say your son is Vofkulak, he preys on our people," said Orphan, as he carved.

"What?" she turned sharply. "Who said so? Why are you spreading this? What has he ever done wrong? He's quiet and obedient. He works hard. And today you're eating his bread. Don't you dare."

The younger brother listened from his corner. He shook his head and screamed wildly.

The door opened and Carver came in, carrying a hare from a trap. He slowly put his prey on the floor, and fell on the bench to catch a breath.

"You're limping," stated Orphan evenly.

"I've fallen from the garret." He took his knife and a wooden piece, and started working.

The next day Orphan headed to the house of the wounded young woman. She was slowly recovering from the wolf's bite. She stood at the front door basking in the autumn sun. Her face was pale, with swollen eyelids and shaking lips. Orphan stood in front of her, watching. The ragged scar went across her neck and did not let her turn her head. She followed Orphan with her eyes. He slowly approached, stroked her dry hair, and touched her bulging scar. She took him by the hand and led him inside.

Darkness seeped into the small house before the shadows cloaked the outside. The young woman's mother lay on the bench; still sick since the night her husband vanished in the woods. There was no food, so they went to sleep on an empty stomach.

❋   ❋   ❋

From his bench, Orphan watches blue slit over the door. Gradually, the color of the outside deepens, melting, sinking into the darkness. In the starless sky, white lightning unfolds and approaches from afar, following an invisible spiral, growing into a gigantic flower, and suddenly blowing up in his closed eyes. He sits upright on the bench, holding his breath. He peers through the darkness, and sees nothing, hears nothing. He breaks into a cold sweat.

❋   ❋   ❋

The workday started early in the hut next door. Twin brothers, the village soap-makers, nude under their leather aprons, hustled around a huge vat, mixing the sticky mass inside. Red embers splashed light onto their bodies, the dark walls, and the barking dogs in cages behind their backs. The dogs were an odd mix, some with two heads, or five legs.

The twins emptied the vat into a bucket on the floor. Thick smoke coated them. One of them handed a shapeless piece of black soap to Orphan.

"Here. This is the largest piece. Give smaller ones to the others. They aren't hunters anyway."

"What do you mean?" Orphan weighed the soap in his hand.

"Old Man said so." The twins came closer and looked into his eyes. "He said you are the one. You have to kill Vofkulak. Our community raised you. You have to serve the community."

One by one, villagers came through the door to receive their soap. Orphan felt their cold fingers, taking pieces of soap from his hands.

"You must," said one of them.

"I know," Orphan said. "I don't mind. Why do you speak to me like this? We will all do it together, won't we?"

"That's right, all together," they said. "Don't fear. You just lure him out of his hut. Give him the soap to smell. It'll drive him crazy. He'll try to hunt you, so he'll turn into a wolf. Then we'll kill him."

The villagers went away. One man stayed behind. He put his hand on Orphan's shoulder, and whispered in his ear.

"Don't listen to them. It is not true. Old Man said Vofkulak couldn't be killed while he's a wolf. Nothing penetrates his iron skin. He must turn human to be killed. And he can only turn human if he gets enough human blood. From here." He touched Orphans neck. "You'll lure him with this soap all right, and then he'll bite your neck and drink your blood, and then he'll turn into a human. That's when they can kill him. That's the only way. That's how you will serve the community."

Orphan stood in the middle of an empty street, deep in thought. A gusting wind almost pushed him down. The first heavy drops of rain fell. He took a few steps, but stopped, startled. The wind suddenly died out. The street was silent. He heard something approaching from afar. He heard the breathing. The back of his head felt the gaze, two burning red eyes staring at him. He was afraid to turn his head to meet those eyes, so he just stood there frozen. Then he slowly turned his head and saw the iron wolf running toward him. As if in a dream, Vofkulak approached, and suddenly turned around, and disappeared in a whirlwind. Sounds rushed in. High winds mixed with the cold rain again, tearing Orphan's cloths away, spitting in his face.

Carver's mother sat at the table with her sewing. Orphan stood before her holding an iron hook with a knotted cord, wagging it back and forth.

"This cannot kill him." He said. "Every night people hunt him with this. They just kill each other with these hooks. It doesn't work."

"It'll work," she said. "He's afraid of the soap. If you give him some dog fat's soap to sniff he'll weaken, and then you can kill him with the hooks."

"Look, woman," Orphan shook his head. "Do you really think I'm that dumb? Is it because I had no mother and nobody to teach me? I'm telling you, this soap is wasted. It doesn't work!"

"How am I supposed to know?" The woman said defensively. "I only heard what Old Man said. I don't know how to kill Vofkulak."

"You do," insisted Orphan. "And you're going to tell me. Otherwise I'll burn your hut, and no one will help you. You know that. I have to die because of your son, so why should I spare you? People say you know how to kill Vofkulak. Tell me. He's our enemy. He killed your son, he drank his blood, and became him. Don't you understand? You are taking Vofkulak for your son. He is not your son Carver anymore. He's a werewolf, and he'll kill us all."

Tears streamed down her face.

"I told you, you must tease him with the soap, and then strike his neck with an iron hook. You can't look him in the eye or turn your back to him, or he'll turn into a wolf and kill you."

"You don't know what you're saying. Old Man said he could not be killed as a wolf. I have to let him bite my neck and taste my blood. Then he can be killed."

"Don't trust them, son," she said. "Do as I say. You have to come up to him when he's a human. Give him some soap to smell. His eyes will turn red. Don't look at him. Don't turn your back to him. Just kill him."

"I can kill him and stay alive? You've given me hope, mother. He stole your son. I'll be your son now. I'll take proper care of you after it's over. Bye, Mother."

He left. She sat on the bench, staring at the door.

The young woman was standing at her front door, looking at the dim autumn sun. Orphan approached her and slowly stroked her hair. She took his hand and led him inside. Her old mother lay sick and delirious in the far corner. Orphan sat on the bench, his back to the table, pulling the young woman to his lap. He stroked and tickled her, whispering in her ear.

"He is as big as a mountain, and as scary as death."

"He is big and scary," she repeated absently.

"He is big and scary. He has iron skin, red eyes, and many legs." He pressed her harder, jerking her shoulders.

"O-o-h, let me go!" She screamed, trying to bite his hand. He didn't let go, covering her mouth with his hand. She was kicking trying to escape, but his strong hands pressed her tighter, never letting go.

The sky hung gray and dead over the silent woods. On a glade among dry leaves, stumps, and shrubs, a dead body blended into the landscape. Carver came by with a load of dry wood on his back. He looked at the corpse. An iron hook was stuck in its neck. He tried to take the dead man's shoes, but he could not pull them off. He took the axe from the dead hand and slowly made his way downhill to the village.

In Old Man's hut, Orphan sat at the table in a clean shirt. Every villager was to stop by with a ceremonial gift—a handful of grain. They approached one by one, pouring the grain in a big bowl, repeating each time, "You die for our salvation."

❦   ❦   ❦

In utter darkness a whirlwind grows fast and approaches with bright lightning, loud thunder, exploding in blinding white blossoms. Orphan opens his eyes and sits straight on the bench. Holding his breath, he looks through the darkness. Everything is silent and quiet. Old Man's little girl sleeps on the other bench. Orphan lies down again, he squeezes his eyes shut, trying to ward off the noise that approaches from the deep. The iron wolf runs right at him burning him with his red eyes. Orphan can see his own hands, illuminated in darkness. They hold an axe. He lifts it, and drops the blade between the wolf's eyes. The axe bounces from the werewolf's iron forehead.

Orphan opens his eyes and sits up straight on the bench. He peers into the darkness, and listens. A thick blanket of silence surrounds him. He puts on his shoes, and goes outside. On his way, he picks up an axe from behind the door. He feels light drizzle on his face and hands. Sky appears darker than earth. Tiny drops of rain run down his face. He turns around. The werewolf stands between him and the front door. He raises his axe and soundlessly splits the wolf's body from head to tail. Two halves of the body fall symmetrically on the ground in front of him. In the darkness and shimmering rain, they seem to move. He looks closer. They are moving. Multiple legs scratch and kick the ground. Within moments, each half regenerates, returning to life. Two werewolves stand upright and run away in opposite directions. Orphan opens his eyes and sits upright on his bench.

❦   ❦   ❦

Gray dawn lights up a small window in the young woman's hut. Her mother, frail and thin, lies on the bench. Black spots cover her skin. She whispers in delirium. "Kill the beast. Kill Vofkulak. Kill the werewolf. Kill him." She talks to herself, not hearing her daughter moaning in pain.

The young woman restlessly walks back and forth. She sits, and stands up again, holding her big stomach, looking around senselessly. She is struggling to overcome the pain that possesses her body. She falls on her knees, lies down, and rolls on the floor. Her scream comes out like a squeak. Her lips tremble and turn bluish. Her mouth, missing teeth, is open wide in a seizure. She gives birth to a lifeless creature that resembles an animal fetus covered with a white sac.

Almost fainting, she wraps it in a cloth, and opens the door with one hand. It's raining outside. She kneels under an old pine tree and starts digging into the wet and cold soil with her bare fingers. The pit gets deeper, and gradually fills with water. She unfolds the cloth and takes the dead fetus in her hands. Through the sac, it resembles a little wooly dog with a tail. She puts it in the grave, and looks up at the sky. Rain gives way to snow. Heavy wet snowflakes fall from the gray sky and cover her face.

Someone approaches from behind. She feels his gaze and turns around. Carver stands staring in front of him in confusion, as if he does not understand where he is. He comes closer and takes her head in his hands, gently pulling her up, making her stand on her feet. She weeps on his shoulder. He pulls her by the hand. She quietly follows him. In the fresh snow, he caresses her while she watches the white snowflakes from behind his shoulder.

Wet snow melted under the warm wind, and added more darkness to the night. A group of villagers came to the garret hut. They brought along a little girl—the village's only child. They carried shovels, knotted cords and iron hooks, prepared to hunt a werewolf.

They stopped in front of the door and started digging a pit. There were too many of them, so the pit became wider, not deeper. The child stood aside, looking along the street. Suddenly she yelled, "He's coming!" She hid behind someone's back. Down the street, Carver was heading home. He walked into the crowd, and fell into the pit. He slid in the mud, trying to stand up. They threw wet soil at him, yelling, "Die, Vofkulak, die." He was covered with dirt.

"Leave me," he begged. "I don't want…I don't want to…" he suddenly stood up, scaring them away, "…to see you anymore."

They ran away screaming, "Vofkulak, Vofkulak!"

His mother stood in the hut listening to the noise. Her son, covered with dirt, crawled through the door. He crossed the room, and climed to the garret, his hiding place. Later, when everything was quiet, a pebble flew into his window, and a child's voice echoed, "Vofkulak, Vofkulak!" in the darkness of the night.

In the young woman's backyard, snow falls on the grave under the pine tree. The snow piles up so fast, that the little hill starts to grow. It grows faster than the piling snow, finally cracks, and falls apart, giving birth, pushing out a live creature in a sac. When the sac breaks, the creature stands up on its shaky legs. There are too many of them, and they are rooted deep in soil. The creature looks around with its red burning eyes, then pulls its legs from the ground one after another, breaking the roots with a crunch. Half-plant, half-animal, it turns into a werewolf. It licks its iron skin, sniffs the earth, and runs away, leaving deep footprints in the snow.

A crowd gathered again and went to Carver's hut. They stood there, waited, whispered, and shook their heads, and then Orphan approached it and opened the door. There was a knotted cord on his shoulder, and a bloodstained package in his hands. He pressed it tightly against his chest.

"Where?" he asked Carver's mother. She silently pointed to the garret. He climbed upstairs, and reached the roof. A quiet night surrounded him, lit by the dense snow. He looked up. Snow flurries seemed gray against the pale sky. They fell on his face. He opened the door to the garret. It was dark inside. The door creaked loudly. Staggering, he dropped the cord with the hook. It fell down into soft snow. He felt his shoulder. His weapon was gone. He stepped inside. Red wolf's eyes were burning somewhere far up, under the garret roof. He called uncertainly, "Vofkulak?" A muffled wolf's howl came from afar.

Carver came up, and lit a candle in the middle of the empty floor. For a moment, Orphan saw a huge shadow of a wolf's head on the wall, but it was gone as he blinked. Carver stayed behind the candle, looking at Orphan. Above his head, a small window made of red glass shone in the glow of the candle. Orphan stared at it, stunned. For a moment, he forgot why he was there. He looked straight into his enemy's eye, and unfolded his package. He scattered pieces of dog meat around him in a circle. Then he took out a piece of black soap.

"See? This soap is made of dogs. Smell it. This is a smell of your death. This is the end of you, werewolf. We uncovered you. We'll cook you into soap now."

Orphan stepped ahead and tried to reach Carver's face. Carver stepped back, and suddenly froze, looking at the door with glossy eyes. Orphan sharply turned around. The door behind him was shut. The shadow of a wolf's head moved across it. He dropped the soap, and rushed to the door. Carver looked at him and howled like an animal, covering his face. Orphan hurried downstairs to the hut where Carver's mother sat silent, and his crippled brother shook and spat, mumbling. Orphan moved slowly through the room. His face was deadly pale, his eyes wide open, filled with horror. The room grew wider in front of him. The distance to the door increased with his every step. Carver's mother extended an axe to him. The one her son once brought from the woods.

❀   ❀   ❀

He knows that he should not take it, but he does. He goes out the door and stands there, ready. The door opens slowly and quietly. The big wolf's head shows up. The werewolf cannot see him. He sees the iron head, and his hands raise the axe and send it down to the wolf's forehead, splitting it between the eyes. The wolf falls down slowly. White snow falls and falls, covering it. The enemy is dead. Why do they still yell "Vofkulak, Vofkulak?"

❀   ❀   ❀

Orphan remembered how people approached him, how they looked at him, and then ran away, screaming. They pointed at him, "Vofkulak, Vofkulak!"

The street was empty when he woke up. The whole village was empty and silent in white snow. He stood up and walked ahead. Then he stopped, looked back and saw deep footprints right behind him. He made another step, and left another wolf's footprint. He ran ahead, out of the village, out of the forest, out of the mountains. He ran as far as no one had ever before. Only birds watched him from the sky—a little black dot moving in the snow valley beyond the mountains.

❀   ❀   ❀

He walks through the solid snow farther and farther, stopping on a hill. Far below, on the plain he sees a big city, divided into blocks, with long and short streets, and squares, and ponds. It is silent, dark and motionless. He moves faster toward the city, falls in the snow, stands up again, and goes ahead. As he approaches, he sees a dump that replaces a once big city. Broken bricks and cement mixed with glass and plastic, cardboard and rags. Everything around is shapeless, burnt, ruined, torn. Here and there, rusted metal plates with radioactive hazard signs are scattered.

There is no one anywhere. He looks around. Each time he turns his head he feels that he is not alone. Shadows slide along his glance. He thinks of rats, but the shadows are too big. Dogs? He turns in their direction. They disappear. Only rust, and mold, and ruin around. He walks ahead, and stops in front of a crumbled wall. Two carved towers of gray stone point to the sky at the top of it. A red glass window shines between them. He looks at the red glass. Some pieces are missing. He feels animals behind his back, but he cannot take his eyes off the shiny window. He feels danger, but he does not care any more.

A pack of monstrous wolves with burning red eyes attacks him. He falls to the ground never to rise again. Soon bloody snow marks the place where a man once stood. The wolves lick it until the last drop of blood is gone.

The leader of the pack turns and smells the air, then heads along the man's tracks. The wolves gather to follow him. They run away from the ruined city, up along the slope, further and further into the mountains, to the remote isolated village.

The sky hung gray and dead. Snow covered miles and miles of unpopulated earth.

Crawling Through Life, Tanks

After Lenin's Death

Lenin created Comintern to make the world revolution possible. He died in January, right on Kim's birthday. Kim did not cry, because he was a communist, and he just turned twenty-four. Born in 1900, he felt like being an ambassador of the new century: an enthusiastic era of freedom, equality, and brotherhood of all the workers and peasants in the world. Kim was named after his grandfather who was Mongolian, or Korean, or Chinese—it did not matter since communists considered any ethnicity to be part of the dark past. What mattered was one's social class and political correctness. Kim came from a class of peasants, which was not as good as coming from the workers, but at least not as bad as belonging to the "rotten intelligencia."

Later that year the Comintern honored Kim with an important mission. He was sent to South America to educate and direct local communists. Ancient intertribal conflict in the small jungle country had acquired a modern pastiche—hostile parties turned into "communists" and "separatists." The morning after Kim started working with his contact he found himself kneeling on a precipice over a jungle river. A Mauser was pressed against his temple.

"Who helped you? Name him," demanded the aborigine. Kim whispered something and the Mauser returned to its owner's loincloth. The aborigine turned to leave, but suddenly pushed his victim off the precipice. Kim went straight down under water, then came to the surface and swam away. His executioner shot after him once, but missed.

⁂

Not far from the river, jungle yielded to highway. On the side of the road, a short man in a derby hat moved as quickly as the occasional automobile. He was roller skating, carrying a cane and a shabby traveling bag. Soon he reached the capital of the country, a dusty little town with crooked streets, and dropped into a bar. The gramophone played a tango. He looked around and noticed a novice, a fair-haired woman in a silvery dress. Her laugh sounded like a crystal bell. He graciously led her to dance.

"I'm Ginger, from Chicago," she said. "Are you American too?"

"Yeah. My name is Friedman. I used to impersonate Charlie Chaplin in LA. But business was slow. I've been to five surrounding countries since then. Now I've got a regular gig in this bar. By the way, do you mind being adored by a strolling actor? I'm poor."

Ginger laughed sweetly, "I love actors. I would like to be a film actress. My late husband was a capitalist, you know. He left me some money. Now Communism sounds so exciting. So I came here to see communists."

"I thought their nest was in Russia," said Friedman.

"Oh yes, I'd love to go to Russia, but my daughter Violet is only five. She can't travel that far and I have no relatives to leave her with."

After the tango, she turned to leave. He caught her red-nailed fingers, and kissed them lightly, tickling her with his mustache.

⁂

The next day Ginger and Violet both fashionably dressed in low-waist outfits and straw hats, headed to the countryside. There, local communists commandeered a small clay house into a Lenin museum. A line of visitors formed at the gate. It was hot and humid, people stood in line licking their lips and sweating. Ginger felt dizzy. She stepped in the shadow of the building, then timidly approached to peek inside. There was a desk there with Lenin's famous green lamp on it, and a tattered leather sofa, too. Suddenly Ginger envisioned Lenin himself lying on the sofa in his military jacket. His comrade-wife Nadezhda Krupskaya in a faded brown dress and horn-rimmed spectacles was lying side by side with him. Ginger realized she was hallucinating. She stepped back. The heat became unbearable, making Violet cranky, so Ginger grabbed her daughter and left.

It was late when Friedman was strolling back home after his nightly performance in the bar. Fragrant night surrounded him with sights and sounds of splendid jungle greenery. He approached his little hut and bumped into a guy who was trying to nestle into a heap of dry palm leaves by the clay wall. Friedman fearlessly stared at the longhaired young Asian in dirty rags. The guy looked like a teenager and was exhausted, hungry and desperate. He begged for help and shelter in the actor's hut. Softhearted "Charlie Chaplin" let him in. His name was Kim, and the local separatist government wanted him. Friedman assured him that since governments change often in this part of the world, it was worthwhile to wait. A new day could wipe out the separatists.

"Until then you can stay here," he said.

"I lost connection with my contact person," said Kim. "He might already be dead. I have to find a new contact. Maybe I'll have to come out in disguise. Thanks for helping me, comrade."

They shared a bowl of rice and Kim fell asleep on the floor. That is how the strolling actor Friedman befriended a Comintern agent.

❧   ❧   ❧

In the morning, the capital resounded with gunshots. Two dented tanks moved across the square. Fresh leaflets in a local dialect and peppered with exclamation points littered the ground. Communists were in control again, and a group of separatists was taken to the Lenin museum to be executed by a firing squad.

After noon, everything calmed down. Ginger went to the market place much later than usual. It was hot, noisy, and crowded. Fresh crabs died by now, greens weathered, bananas browned. She was lazily picking cured melon, when an Asian girl with a shopping basket attracted her attention. The girl was thin and flat-chested. Her long braided hair shone like a black sun. At first, Ginger decided the girl was someone's maid, but her demeanor was not like that of a servant. She walked graciously, like a tigress. Ginger watched her for awhile trying to figure out what was so disturbing about this strange creature. Suddenly she decided that this girl could be a spy, an enemy of the new communist government. She turned around and hurried to the central square. A red banner waved above the two-story building. She entered and stood in front of the local commissar who was sitting at his desk in a sweaty uniform.

"Most likely I am mistaken," she started awkwardly, "but this person was so strange-looking…this girl I just saw at the market place. I know there are so many enemies around. I just wanted to warn you. It's not like I am sure about it, but I am your supporter. I support communists." The commissar watched her with blood-shot eyes, chin in hand. He nodded doubtfully.

That night Ginger had a date with Friedman. She watched his performance at the bar and laughed. He was charming. She almost fell in love with him, although in general she preferred taller men. Then they danced the tango again. He was a great dancer being as short and light as a woman. They moved so perfectly together that the bar owner put their drinks on the house for the night. At dawn, when the bar was closed, Ginger refused to be taken home. They just laughed and walked, and ended up at Friedman's place. Kim woke up to their loud drunken voices, and hurriedly hid in the pantry. When they walked inside Ginger hugged and kissed Friedman right at the threshold. She tried to take off her dress, but he pulled it up with both hands, aware of Kim's presence somewhere in the dark room. After a short tug-of-war, Ginger's dress became all twisted and wrinkled. Confused and embarrassed, she left.

In the morning at the market place, she ran into the strange girl again. Ginger decided to follow her and watch closely. The girl suddenly turned around looking her straight in the eye. Ginger smiled nervously, "Oh, I'm sorry to be in your way. I couldn't help noticing you for the second time here. Are you new to the town?"

The girl's name was Kim. She was just a traveler in this country all on her own, and so awfully charming and friendly. Soon the two of them were shopping together. They talked and laughed, peeled ripe bananas, and tried coconut milk. Kim was stronger than Ginger, so she helped her to bring her purchases home. They agreed to shop together again. In a few days, they became inseparable. Walking in the jungle with her new friend, Ginger was overcome with unusual attraction to this exotic female. She lowered her voice and asked nervously, "Have you ever kissed a woman, Kim?"

Kim thought about it for a moment, then pulled up his disguising skirt. Ginger laughed so hard, that she fell on the grass, pulling Kim along. They made love in the middle of the emerald greenery. Sunlight sifting through the light and dark leaves above them was gleaming on Kim's long black hair. Ginger's short blond curls jumped up and down like golden shavings covering her cheekbones and revealing them again, tanned and rosy like flower petals. The sun was high and white. Then it changed its angle and became low and golden. Thousands of tiny shadows crossed the shimmering light. Glossy leaves reflected every movement. Ginger could not stop caressing her wonderful lover. Suddenly she remembered her report to the authorities, and started crying.

Kim listened to her confession silently. He stood up, put on his drag outfit and left, brushing against hard and soft branches on his way. Ginger ran after him. In her grief, she did not notice that he walked straight into Friedman's house. She followed him crying and begging forgiveness. They reconciled inside the cool clay hut laughing, crying and kissing each other like crazy. The sumptuous jungle sunset shone in a small dirty window behind their backs.

❧   ❧   ❧

On his day off, Friedman borrowed a car from the bar owner and took Ginger and Violet for a joyride. Communists were patrolling the city. Two dented tanks lumbered around the central square. A group of local tramps, suspected in helping separatists, was escorted to the red-bannered building for a quick trial. Suddenly a skirmish erupted nearby. After the first gunshots rang, the joy riders left the car and fled the square. The fight continued all day and the following night. Separatists took over at dawn. They walked through the city knocking at doors. They took half-dressed men out of their homes and escorted them to the Lenin museum for execution. The museum was badly vandalized—walls spotted with dirt and burn marks, the front yard stained with urine. Gunfire resounded throughout the city. Two tanks continued prowling the streets, but now separatists were doing the steering.

Kim disappeared from Friedman's hut without any explanations. A series of explosions and arsons erupted in the town, turning it into a deserted ruin. The separatist leader was riding around in the bar owner's car with a green-orange national banner attached to the spare wheel on the back.

One morning a bomb killed him, strangely causing very little harm to the car. Power automatically passed to the communists. The red banner returned to the roof of the official building. Kim showed up at Friedman's hut at the end of the day. Friedman, Ginger, and Violet were sitting around the table, for the hundredth time discussing where he could be. Glancing at the door, and seeing Kim there as dirty and exhausted as a stray cat, Ginger screamed and ran to him to hug and hold him tight. Kim gently took her hands off his neck and sat by the table. Ginger cried and hugged him while he gulped his rice.

Through the day different groups of separatists and their supporters were shot in front of the Lenin museum. The reconstruction started immediately after. The wounded commissar in a blood-stained bandage supervised it, fighting his dizziness. He approved the newly arrived plush sofa seized from the separatists, a substitute for the leather one that vanished from the museum. The portrait of Lenin was gone, too. An obscenity marked its place on the wall. Commissar thoughtfully looked around. Then he picked up a brochure, and tore out a portrait of Karl Marx. Overcome with giddiness, he took scissors and cut off Marx's long locks. Then he shortened Marx's beard and wedge-shaped it. He sighed, and painstakingly wrote LENINA under the cropped Marx portrait, adding an extra letter to Lenin's name, perhaps just out of delirium. He looked at his work with satisfaction, and proudly glued it to the wall.

Late that night an urgent council meeting took place at Friedman's hut. Kim was restless. Communists were at power again, but the commissar did not know how Kim's solo-terrorist acts helped to gain victory. All his contacts were dead. Somewhere in the commissar's desk, Ginger's report on him was filed. Should he show up, the trial would be quick and unjust. He did not think it was wrong. In war circumstances communists were supposed to act fast. It is just that he was not ready to die. Kim decided to leave and get back to Moscow. He would report to Comintern. They would send him somewhere else. Ginger cried on his shoulder like a little girl. But he made his decision.

Next morning they all drove in the bar owner's dented car to the state border deep in the jungle. Kim shook Friedman's hand, kissed Ginger and Violet, and crossed the border marked with green and orange lines on tree trunks. He continued walking through the same jungle in the direction of the same highway, only in a different, capitalist country, not yet touched by progressive movements. "The victory of the world revolution is unavoidable," said Lenin in one of his famous speeches. So one day all these countries shall become communist under the power of workers and peasants. This thought made Kim march merrier ahead. Sunspots ran over his shiny black hair. Friedman's roller skates hung over his shoulder. He will put them on once he reaches the highway. In the next capital, he will find out about the ship. He touched Ginger's gift in his pocket, a tiny silvery purse filled with rolled up bank notes. A long long trip to Moscow lay ahead.

They sat silently in the car. Then Ginger said, "I have to go, too. I have to follow him. He does not want it now, but he will later. He does not realize that he needs me. I want to be there for him when he will look for me. Do you understand?"

"Yeah," said Friedman looking aside, both hands on the steering wheel.

"We will be happy there, Kim and I."

"And if not?"

"If not, then I'll come back. I'll find you both and we'll live together. Right, baby?"

"Right, Mom," said Violet, absorbed with the actor's watch on a thick faux silver chain. "We'll be waiting for you…"

After Stalin's Death

…After Stalin's death in 1953, among the political prisoners set free from the zone, there was an old stooped Asian, dry and wrinkled as a mummy, with gray bristle on his cheeks. His guard teased him, "Say American spy, how did you survive a twenty-five years sentence? You are one year short, right. Aren't you lucky, that the Master died?" The old man just grinned, not a single tooth left in his gums. The guard opened the gate and continued, "I remember the accomplice in your case. That Hollywood blond. If you hadn't dragged her along they never would have exposed you. Women. Bitches! They are killing us. You stupid American spy. But she paid her price. It's been like twenty years since she bit the dust. See that cellblock? Right there. 'Of heart failure' if you know what I mean."

The prisoner stood beyond the gate, frozen under the blazing sun.

Glossary

Run Your G-string Up The Flagpole And See If It's Perestroika

Perestroika (Russian)—Rebuilding, reorganizing. Started in 1986, perestroika led to the fall of the Soviet Union. Perestroika represents the period in Russian history that ended Communism.
Pobeda—A Soviet car produced after WWII.
Pravda—The leading Communist party newspaper.
Volga—The official car of Soviet V.I.P.'s.

Vofkulak

Vofkulak (Ukrainian)—Werewolf.

Crawling Through Life, Tanks

Comintern—An abbreviation for the Communist International organization.
Lenin—The first leader of the Communist party and the founder of the Soviet Union. 1870-1924.
Stalin—General Secretary of the Communist party and leader of the Soviet Union from 1922 to 1953.

About the author

Emma Krasov, a graduate of Kiev State University, has published her poems in Ukrainian literary magazines since she was 16. She worked as a screenwriter, movie critic, and journalist. A play of hers was performed on stage in Kiev and other Ukrainian cities. She has written lyrics to songs performed on the radio and in films. Her articles and film reviews have appeared in both Ukrainian and Russian newspapers and magazines. In 1992, she moved to the United States and lived in Chicago for 9 years. There, she published a Russian-language newspaper, *Contact*, and taught a class "Russian Cinema 1980–1990: Reel Life and Personal Affairs During Perestroika" in the Facets Multi-Media Cinematheque. She also worked as an exhibit developer for the Field Museum. She wrote an article "A Timeline of Russian Political History," included in a book *Kremlin Gold*, published by Harry N. Abrams, Inc. Recently, she moved to an obscure location in California, and now enjoys the weather as she works on her new book.

0-595-22384-2